BENINO THE DARK OF DAYS

Book II of the Gräzland Tales

*Published by gracious permission of
The Council of Three
and the College of the King*

Adapted by Jayceson Talewright
Translated by Trevor V.W.

Copyright © 2018 Trevor Van Winkle

All rights reserved. This book or any portion thereof may not be reproduced or used in any manner whatsoever without the express written permission of the publisher except for the use of brief quotations in a book review.

ISBN-13: 978-1721523580
ISBN-10: 1721523588

Any references to historical events, real people, or real places are used fictitiously. Names, characters, and places are products of the author's imagination.

Second printing, 2018.

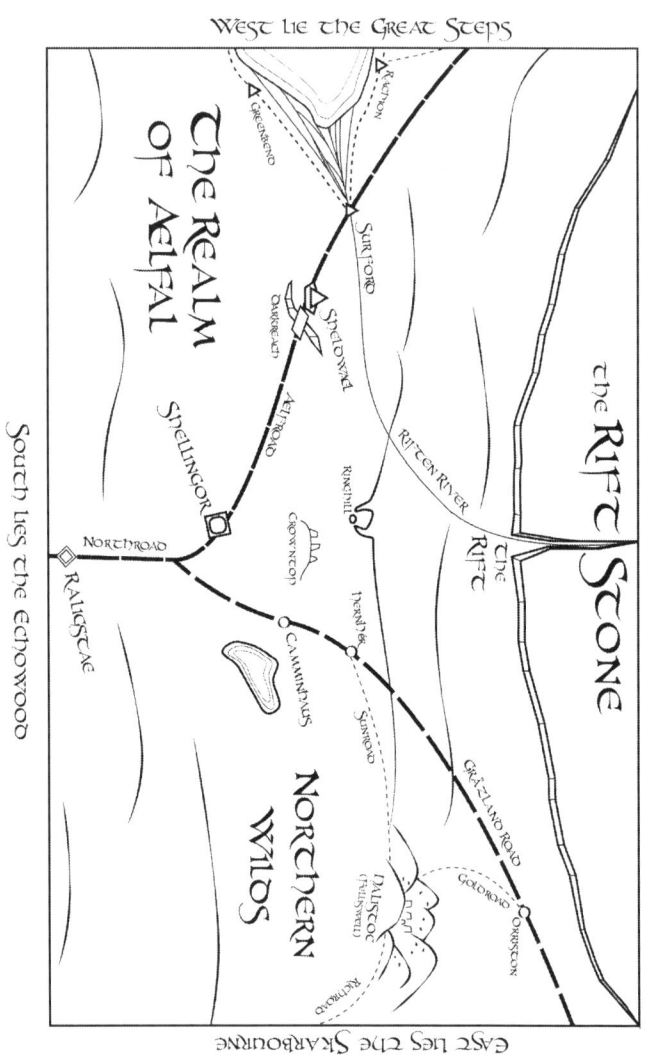

Map of the Northern Borderlands

West lie the Great Steps

the Rift Stone

South lies the Echowood

East lies the Skarbourne

- Raeton
- Greenbend
- Surford
- Darkreach
- Sheltowne
- Aelrood
- Rinothill
- Ritten River
- The Rift
- Shellingor
- Crow Neop
- Northroad
- Thornheic
- Raligstae
- Camminhius
- Sunford
- Grazeland Road
- Dalescoc (Trentswell)
- Goldenoo
- Orrkseon
- Ragtroad

The Realm of Aelfal

Northern Wilds

captivum solve Israel

I

They've taken the prince.

There: if I get nothing else down in this little pamphlet, those words will bear witness against my captors, should I not make it home – as seems ever-more likely. They won't do me much good – my captors are the only ones who know this book exists. Exhillion, at least, knew of my last journal… though this one isn't half so generous as that book, used up with fearful writing. It's little better than a practice book, like the ones Obris had me use. Ha! Those always came back written-over with corrections; the eyes reading over my shoulder now, already so full of judgement, make me fear it will share the same fate. At least he read that bold opening and didn't snatch the book away. Guess I'll go on, then.

I remember dreaming again last night: walking down the empty road with springtime dying around me. The clanking and the rustling and the snapping of black cloth grew louder and louder. I pulled against invisible cords which seemed to hold my neck in place. I caught the shoulder of a night-black robe at the edge of my vision… and woke, bolting upright in bed.

Or rather I would have; the horrible paralysis which sometimes chases dreams sat heavy on my chest. My heart hammered beneath the weight as I tried to breath, breath, *breath*… but the weight refused to fade. And it wasn't just on my chest, either; the air felt heavy across my entire body, pressing me into the mattress. I breathed again, slower and deeper. Thin steam met the frigid air, then rippled like water in the pale light. The ceiling stared back at me. I lay on my back, unable to see much of the room… but in the corner of my eye, something stirred: a dark shape, moving past my bed.

I screamed. At least, I tried to scream: my mouth opened and thick, heavy air poured down my throat, cold as lake water. My fear that dreams had somehow breached the waking world was overshadowed by a new panic – I was drowning, a hundred miles from the sea. The shape turned in the dark, and I made out the wide, black brim of a hat against the curtain. It raised one long, pale finger to its lips (or what I presumed were lips). The sound which followed was too much like the hiss of a snake, but still all-too-human: a signal for quiet. Beneath the broad rancher's hat, I caught sight of two glimmering blue eyes before the figure turned back to rummaging through my pack.

Mage-Addict! was my first thought. Of course it was: the glowing eyes, the dark clothes, the magyk suffocating me as they searched through my supplies for more of the stuff – or failing that, coin to buy it. My second thought came screaming in just after: *The prince!* He was still on the nightstand; unguarded, unhidden, and the thief had just come from that direction. His secondvessel looked dull and insignificant; without the aid of the drug, I doubt it could even be seen in the dark. But if they looked closer, and saw the gemstones glittering in the crest…

My third thought trailed, a little slower than the others: *What if they're looking for him?* I'd long dismissed the king's fears of Ælfali spies, but if the half-seen creature rummaging through my pack was an ælf… I hadn't seen their ears when they stood silhouetted against the dawnlight, but their hat would've hidden them – from me, and from anyone else who might've taken offense at the presence of ælfkind in the stronghold of man. If Ælfal had learned of Alexi's death and sent a spy (or worse, an assassin) to claim his ashes, I was a dead man – I, and half the Vale with me. Had I but a moment to think, I would've realized it couldn't be so; ælfs don't use ~~the maj~~ magyk.

My reader (my captive audience, backwards as the phrase may be) made me cross out the Warden-slang. Guess he'll be doing more than reading after all. ~~Arches. Arches~~? Fine.

I didn't get a moment to think: the shadow rose again, slinging its satchel 'round one shoulder. A sense of familiarity rose with them: the shape of their hat, the cut of their cloak… I felt certain I knew them, but I couldn't place the feeling. The figure reached out, pressing a spiderish finger into the hollow of my chest. The drowning air thinned and disappeared. Suddenly free, I tried to scream for Brook; forgetting he'd already left me behind. Someone else might've heard me, though – but all I got out was a wheeze like a man with lung-flu. My chest felt like it'd been crushed by a wayward hay bale for the second time in a week. My arms and legs lay heavy as stones and limp as wet corn stalks, though the paralysis was gone. Running was out, but I could finally turn my head. I took the easiest course, letting it fall towards the window, the intruder, and (most importantly) the nightstand. Even that felt like moving a millstone. Something filled my throat again, but this time it had naught to do with magyk. The prince was gone.

I didn't see if my journal was still there; I was too distracted to notice. I don't know what's become of that volume – the only record of the dark doings of Raligstae – but I hope it wasn't left in that room. Or maybe I hope it was.

In any case, the prince was gone, and his spindly thief-kidnapper was hauling me to my feet. Whoever they were, they were stronger than they looked, thanks to ~~the maj~~ magyk. Managing to sit me up, they sat beside me on the bed (carefully keeping their bag from being crushed between us) and slung my arm over their shoulder. Pushing up with a muted groan, they stood to their full height, pulling me up with them. My head lolled forward: all I could see were the hardy, dirt-crusted boots of my captor and my own stockinged feet, dragging useless on the floorboards as we made for the door. I was unable to help, even if I wanted to. I did try to struggle, but I doubt they even noticed; all I could do was set my dead weight against our course. We hardly lost a step.

The door opened of its own accord, creaking far less than when I'd opened it. We stumbled into the third story hall; a small, glass lamp at one end banished total darkness. Realizing my chance, I turned to look at my captor's face (my head still feeling like a bag of bricks), but they had already turned back towards my room – parlor, I mean. Their scarecrow arm (the one not pinned to my side) rose, knobbled knuckles popping as they snapped. Blue sparks flashed in the corner of my vision. I craned my neck further. My backpack was ablaze, the maps and charts feeding it like so much kindling. My eyes went wide, and shock made me forget to hold my head up. It knocked against my kidnapper's skull as we both turned back. The hallway dimmed, and their shoulders sagged; I dared to hope they'd topple to the floor. Alas, no favor from Lady Fortune; the thief sucked air through their teeth, straightened, and started for the end of the hall. Last I saw of my parlor (which I didn't need to pay for after all), the flames, blue and unnaturally bright, caught the corner of the itchy wool blankets.

I wonder if the guests on the floor above made it out in time – I can only hope they fled before the fire stabbed its fingers into the ceiling.

Those on the third floor (far fewer than the innkeeper had implied) got ample warning. We were halfway down the passage before the smoke began tickling my nose. As we neared the exit, my eyes started to sting. The kidnapper-arsonist stopped a few feet from the door, turned, and cried *Fire! Fire!* as loud as they could. The words seemed to echo in the quiet dark for a long, breathless moment, then the doors burst open behind us. Footsteps hammered on the carpet. Other voices picked up the call, one after another, until it was impossible to say who'd said it first. I barely heard any of that, though: my feelings of recognition came home with the first shout. That voice... *his* voice...

It had been raised in quite a different call the night before, as the student made his loud toast in the commons. Before that, it had raised the very same words in a very different room... Capital keep, that is. I lifted my eyes, finally seeing his face. I'd seen it once before, in the kitchens beneath the castle, where he'd ordered me to turn my pockets out. Every other time I might've glimpsed it – in the darkened corners of Raligstae and Shellingor (and maybe even Gillerhern) – its features were hidden beneath his wide, dark hat. A pentaform glittered gold in the shadows despite his attempt to tuck it under his lapels; too sanctimonious to leave it behind, I suppose, though I'm sure he'd prefer to call it reverence.

The revelation was too much. My chin fell back onto my chest as several guests pushed us out of the way, racing down the stairs in varying states of undress. Others rushed back into their rooms, calling for canteens, chamber pots, blankets... anything to smother the flames. I presumed they were soldiers, Wardens, or fools: I've known few smallfolk who'd even consider such a brave, vain course. I wouldn't – but then again, I knew the fire was a mage-flame. They burn like ill-tempered oil fires, and quenching them just makes them madder. The firestarter-father needed a diversion for his kidnapping scheme. He picked the most extreme.

We'd reached the door. A well-meaning fellow, stocky as a dwarfish and twice as tall, stopped to help us as the air began to grow warm. The man, bigger than Brook (if not so well-built) and sporting the ruddy beard and arms of a lumberman, took my right arm over his shoulders and lifted with the priest, hauling me down the stairs. My toes dragged and fell, dragged and fell as they played the part of drinking partners to a too-heavy drunk. We must've looked like the Wardens who'd stumbled down the Kingshead's steps when I first arrived.

My feet were so bruised by the time we passed the keeper's desk I doubted I'd ever stand again. Alarm continued to grow as new voices picked up *Fire! Fire!* on the floors above. The guests, half-asleep or quickened by fear, poured into the commons. Whoever chose to stack the inn so high clearly hadn't been thinking of fire half so much as profit: the stairwell was fast becoming a chimney.

I managed to raise my head towards the crowd. A terror-blind mob filled the tavern, four dozen strong and clawing for the door just wide enough for three. One man took a violent swing at his neighbor, who scampered back. I saw no more. My head was too heavy to hold up, but the whistle of air and the crunch of bone told the rest. *Make Way!* the woodsman cried, with all the deluded conviction of someone trying to save a life. The clambering ahead stopped dead. As we crossed the spit-polished oaks of the common room floor, stockings and bare toes passed by on either side. No one resisted us at the front door.

Our unlikely trio – the arsonist-holy man, the kidnapped farmer, and the unknowingly-complicit giant – went across the porch, down the steps (each a fresh toe-battering for me) and over the narrow road quicker than words... quicker than my words, at least. Not that the alley would long be safe from the fire, but it was safe enough for the moment – the woodsman thought so, at least. He took my full weight, lifted me onto the porch of the building opposite the Kingshead (the tailor's shop?) and leaned me against the railing. My head fell back against the post with a loud thump, but I hardly felt it: I could finally see the smoke.

It poured poison from the third story windows; not just from mine, shattered by the heat, but the entire row. Glowing tendrils of red and blue reached for the rooms above. The guests, fire-fighting Wardens included, poured out of the inn like rats from a sinking ship. Guess those heroes finally realized the futility. A few people stared gap-gawed in the middle of the street at the tinderbox they'd all been sleeping in a moment before. It was fast transforming into a picture of the lowest Arches.

Huh... guess it's okay to write *Arches*, so long as I'm not swearing. Good to know.

The wiser ones (mostly those wearing uniforms) ran for the safety of uptown... safety for the moment, at least. Fires spread faster than thought in the cities.

The woodsman, staring up at the blaze, turned back and knelt to check my eyes for signs of smoke-poisoning. The dark priest watched, eyes shining out of the shadows 'cross his face. My face hung limp as a banner on a windless day; I couldn't so much as grimace. I tried, like Brook, to burn words into the air: *Help me!* I stared, ~~For Heaven's sake~~, *Help Me!* (Oh, so that's blasphemous? Perfect.) No words appeared – and even if they had, they would've been selfish. My eyes should've written *Run! Run you fool... he's right behind you!*

The priest had crept up without a sound, but I must've made some sign when I saw him; the woodsman raised an eyebrow, then turned to face him. He opened his mouth, probably meaning to ask what happened... but nothing came out. The priest reached out, as though to shake his hand in thanks – then tapped him, ever-so-lightly, on the chest. Beneath his hat, his eyes flared brighter, and the giant stopped, tottered, and toppled. My head fell forward as he did: he landed on his face, blood pouring from his nose to stain the dirt a deeper red.

Oh? My reader (a more impatient audience than I would've liked) insists the man was fine; that he conjured heavy air beneath him to slow his fall. I'm grateful if he did – even if it was just to muffle the sound.

The priest stepped over the man (at least half again over his height and weight) and hefted me to my feet, dragging me towards the crowd. Men and women fled the neighboring buildings as it became clear the fire wouldn't stop with the Kingshead. Embers landed on the thatched roof of the blacksmith's, setting it ablaze. Horses and mules screamed in the stables as I was pulled along, following the people of the fortress city as they fled the enemy within their walls. Like fish in a dike, my captor and I were carried through the alleyways and back into the main avenue. Even so far from the inn, the commotion had wakened the city. My head was less heavy by then, and I saw more of the citizens (more than their feet, anyways), dressed in naught but their nighties as they gawked at the flames and rising smoke.

Most, at least, looked that way: calculating how long they had before the fire reached their homes (not long)… but not all of them. Some – not many, but a good few – seemed hardly to notice the fire. Their eyes were fixed on another strange, terrible sight, further down the street. Noticing the crowd gathering 'round the Warden barracks, I craned my neck towards it. I couldn't make sense of what I saw: City-Wardens, a full troupe of them, stood outside the double doors with crossbows in hand – not the bolt-throwers Brook used, but the heavy, full-laden arms of the Capital guard. Two sheriffs stood to either side of the gate, long, cruel pikes leveled at some unseen person within. They all seemed unused to the weapons, but nothing in their bearing suggested they'd find difficulty in using them should the need arise. A pack of cadets held the small but growing crowd back with hard words and the occasional hard shove. The whole scene felt so un-Warden-like, playing out in front of their headquarters as it did. I thought maybe they'd captured some outlaw in the wild: a dangerous felon who needed to be removed from their sanctum. I was almost right.

The prisoner stepped out into the reddened light. The archers gripped their unfamiliar weapons tighter. Two Wardens held him by his arms; their commander followed, lean and tall with a velvet cape draped over his uniform – hardly Warden-fashion, to my eyes. Their captive was red faced and bleeding from a dozen cuts, sustained in some recent struggle. Chains held his wrists in the small of his

Book II

back, connected to fetters on his ankles and a collar 'round his neck by further chains. They looked excessively tight and heavy... yet somehow seemed insufficient to hold the man they bound. I would know: above the iron noose, beneath the blood and bruises and swollen flesh, was the face of my once-called friend.

Brook was rearing to fight. The all-too-familiar fire burned behind his eyes, visible even down the street... or maybe that was just the Kingshead fire? Even so, he didn't struggle to free himself. Strategy had been beaten into him as a cadet, and I could almost hear him counting the weapons surrounding him in his head. This was not the time or place for an escape, and he knew it.

I lacked his discipline. Hope rushed in over reason when I saw him, and I tried to shout his name again, forgetting the dry hollow feeling in my chest. Something – a squeak, perhaps – got out above the noise of the crowd... but he heard it. Brook turned my way. Through the mob and fire and my own ~~damnable~~ weakness, he heard my voice. He turned his fearsome figure, took a half step towards me... then took a baton to the skull. The captain lowered his weapon.

Brook didn't topple. He stopped mid-step, scowled, and turned back towards the officer with an annoyed look. The captain raised his club again, taking a worried step backwards as Brook leaned forward... then collapsed, unmoving.

I heard a voice call for more men to lift the sixteen stone of unconscious Warden – but I saw no more. My captor's eyes flashed in my periphery, and what strength I had left failed. My head fell back to my chest; if anything, I felt weaker than I had at the start. The priest turned for the south gate. It glared back at him, wide, spiked, and sealed fast. Why we were going that way with such haste (as much haste as he could muster, with the magyk starting to run out) escaped me. It was nearing morn, but the doors wouldn't open 'til truedawn... still an hour hence. And how did the priest get through them in the first place? He was back in Raligstae with Brook and I the day before – I know he entered the Kingshead after me last night. He'd been following me, perhaps since I left the Capital... and none too close, if he'd kept the Warden from smelling him and his hateful magyk. The gates had practically closed on our heels as we entered, so how (*how?*) had he entered the city?

Apparently, he apparated through the city wall – at least, that's what he's claiming now. I've heard some priests boast that they can do that: turn the Vale on its axis and push themselves through walls. Honestly, I think it's less of a stretch to say some city watchman will be feeding his family a bit better than normal for the next few weeks... if they still have a table to eat off of.

An alarm bell sounded from the northeast tower, joined quickly by those in the other three. From the battlements, horns rose in an ear-splitting wail. If anyone in Shellingor was still sleeping, they weren't anymore. Above the tumult I heard (or rather felt) heavy iron boots running past us. A moment later, there came grunting and the scrape of wood over iron as the crossbeam was lifted free. Hinges big as bookcases groaned as half-giant soldiers strained at the doors. Panicked murmurs turned to cheers, and I felt the air moving 'round us as the Shellingorians rushed out, desperate to put the walls between themselves and the blaze. The priest didn't rush – he didn't need to. We slipped through the gates just as they opened wide enough. As in the commons, no one got in our way. I'm glad the fortress city still shows such kindness to strangers.

It was darker outside the walls than in, despite the sun glimmering on the horizon beneath a high sheet of cloud. I made another effort to look up and saw the crowd gathering some fifty feet down the road, where the smoke could be clearly seen. My eyes were quickly drawn away from them. A half-cart, hitched to an ancient-looking ass with a mangy grey coat and a mop of black hair, sat to the side of the road. It wasn't so unlike the wagon Jayceson and I hired every year:

simple, cheap, and old – though I doubted that the checkered quilt across the back concealed cabbages. The creature at the end of the reins gave a muted whinny: they'd muzzled their mule. Its mane matched the hood and dark cloak of its driver. Like my captor, he was slight and bony, hidden by the dusk as he sat on the wagon's bench... but he, too, seemed terribly familiar. I had no trouble recognizing his cloak: it was identical to the ones worn by the other priests in the Capital. When he turned his boyish face into the firelight creeping from the gate, I had no trouble recognizing it either; it wore the same anxious expression it had in the Raligstae chapel. Guess I was right to suspect the young acolyte.

The reins jittered and shook in his hands, and I saw sweat shining beneath his hood in spite of the chill. His eyes lit as he saw us approaching; if the layer of frost on the blanket was any sign, he'd been waiting there all night... he was more than ready to go. Me? I could've tarried a while... perhaps long enough for someone to notice the strange goings-on outside their gates. Again, Dame Fortune didn't smile so kindly: the fire held the attentions of everyone in Shellingor, watchmen included.

The priest-kidnapper slid my arm off his shoulder as he dumped me into the bed of the cart, taking just enough time to prop me against the side rail before turning to fuss with the tarp. He spent a few minutes struggling with the heavy, dingy patchwork of colorful cotton, wool, and goodness knows what else. I turned my head as he worked. The assembly down the road all looked more or less in our direction; one even caught my gaze, returned a shy smile, then looked back up in terrified awe before I could signal my distress. No one took me for anything more than a lounger in the back of his friend's wagon – never mind that the wagon had clearly been lying in wait since before the fire started. They had other matters to distract them. Unless...

There was one way. Even without Brook's training, I thought the chance at escape was decent – perhaps the only chance I'd get. The priest, just finishing with the tarp, exchanged some hushed and hurried words to comfort his nervous follower. Slowly – ever-so-carefully – I did one of the few things left within my power: fall. My plan (no masterstroke, but elegant enough for the likes of me) was easy as anything… I'd done it often enough by accident, and seen others do the same. Someone would rush over to help me; they had to. I didn't even need to worry about losing my nerve – I couldn't catch myself, even if I tried.

And I didn't – some other force took hold of me before I could, arresting, then reversing, my fall. I was back upright before I knew what was happening. Still it kept pulling. I fell again… backwards, slower, and quieter than I'd planned. The walls of Barrow-stone sank in my vision. The fattening smoke, glowing red and orange, appeared and disappeared. The last morning stars twinkled above as my head thumped down on the rough boards of the cart-bed. The priest, holding the sheet aloft with one hand, rested the other on the rail as he looked down at me.

His eyes, still glowing in the fading dark, turned towards the Shellingorians with a look I didn't much like… though I liked the one he gave me even less. "I don't expect much company on the road today," he said, "but if we do meet anyone, try not to make any noise." He didn't give me a reason. He didn't need to. My imagination did his work for him.

The curtain fell over me, a suffocating darkness worse than the magyk in the Kingshead; at least that hadn't itched so fiercely. Leather snapped against horseflesh, and the mule gave a muted bray before the cart rolled forward: up and over the curb, then down and off it a moment later. I tried not to cry out. Every bump in the road jolted and bruised me, already pack-sore and stiff from sleep and cold. Lying flat on my back and strengthless, there was nothing I could do to lessen the blows. Even when the spell began to fade (two torturous cross-country hours later), I dared move only enough to curl into a ball. The priest's non-threat wasn't the sort of thing I easily forgot.

Had I been riding any other way, I might've welcomed a day off my feet... maybe even been rocked to sleep by the sway of the wagon. Lying in the bed of the cart, however, with splintery planks for a mattress and an itching quilt for sheets, I stayed well and wide awake. Mindless fear of what waited at our journey's end grew with every mile. Beatings? Torture? Death? We'd just descended a rolling wildland hill and begun to climb another when the acolyte called a *whoa* to his unfortunate animal. Tired of hauling the three of us along, he gratefully obliged. The cart rocked sideways; someone had just jumped off. I coiled tighter beneath the tarp, ready (I thought) for anything. The blanket flew free; daylight, only slightly dimmed by sunset, screamed into my eyes. I threw my arms against it, fearing some last terrible bit of magyk and then – the Dreamlands.

"Hullo there, farmer!" a child's voice called out of the white-hot haze.

My eyes were slow to adjust, but they eventually made out the shape of a broad, boyish smile on a round, hairless face. I leapt up, realizing I was defenseless – and regretted every old bone in my back as I did. The acolyte (whose name I've yet to learn) jumped back too, clutching the pentaform at his neck. It still hung open and empty as it'd been in Raligstae. Neither of us moved for a long while.

The elder priest was far less friendly than his follower – as should be expected. He'd doffed his cap, exposing the harsh line of his bare temple and tapered scalp to the merciless sun. He marched to the center of our soon-to-be camp without a glance in my direction, examined the spot for a moment... then fell to his knees. He dropped so quickly I was almost worried for him – almost. Maybe he'd consumed too much of the holy stuff. His disciple noticed the look in my eyes. He turned, then chuckled; "He's fine, farmer," he said, simple smile returning, "just praying, that's all."

And so he was – praying, that is, and for the better part of an hour. The acolyte made camp while I stood a ways off, sulking beside a spire of rock at the hillock's edge. The last red rays of day met the first silver streams of night as the sun westered. The archer's moon bent over a rolling white plain, heavy with snow for leagues on end. The low rise where we made our camp – a frozen hill ringed with sharp, dark points of stone – was the only landmark besides our tracks. Those vanished over the far-off horizon, and, just beyond that, a thin blue line of smoke caught the last of the sunlight. When day finally failed, the flatlands glowed cold and empty in the moonlight. I shouldn't have worried so much about drawing passers-by: we'd come to a place fit only for thieves and kidnappers… or their victims.

My hand rested on the smooth, cool stone. In truth, my whole weight rested on it; I barely felt strong enough to stand. It wasn't the spell (long-faded), or even the day in the cart (over and done with) which stole my strength. It was the sight of the dead lands below, devoid of farmhouses, cottages, or even Warden-cabins. In the silent stillness, question after question raced screaming through my mind: *Why did they take me? What were they planning? Was this a kidnapping? Arrest? Execution? What were they waiting for? And* (and this one still hasn't gone away) *where was my journal?*

No answer for that, eh Kirlinder? ~~Damn~~.

I'd been mooning over the lonesome wilds so long I was nearly snoring on my feet when a hand clamped all-too-eagerly onto my shoulder. I must've left my skin behind as I jumped. The acolyte (as panicked as I was) jumped too… in a far safer direction; the ridge of the hill, and the sheer drop beyond, were at my feet. I tripped on a snowdrift, turned my ankle, and slid down the cold, cold, *cold* hillside. The snow slid up, into my jacket, shirt, and trousers – thankfully, it stayed out of my boots. I glared up at him with all the gratitude of a housecat on bath day. The boy managed to turn both red and pale all at once. "Fire's ready," he squeaked before scampering away.

A warm fire, a lukewarm supper, and a new journal (if you can call a ream of ribbon-wrapped hemp paper such); those were the things waiting for me at journey's end. If I'd known that, then maybe I would've stolen a few winks of sleep during the ride. The acolyte was fussing with something in the cart by the time I limped, shivering, to the flames. The old sorcerer was rising from his prayers, knees wet, face unsmiling. I turned and set my cold back towards the heat; thankfully, that also put it towards my captor. He could've done better with the fire… I've seen his earlier work up close, after all. Without magyk, the stack of straw and kindling-branches would've barely burned for an hour – not stacked that way, at least. For all his grim scowls and hardy garb, he's just a city priest. These are the wilds: the domain of the Wardens. I doubt he even knows how to strike a flint.

Thinking about Wardens brought Brook (and the much warmer fire we'd once shared) back into my mind. The image of him, bloody and battered and wrapped in chains, felt like a dream which wouldn't fade with daybreak. Kirlinder (the arsonist-father watching me write) must've seen my brow knit with confusion – or else read my thoughts, as some priests claim to do.

"Thinking about your friend?" he asked. His tone wasn't so different from Brook's, come to think of it: the question didn't sound like a question at all. "The Warden?" he added, when I refused to answer.

Brook. I kept my back to him as I spat the name out like a curse. I had nearly dried out by then (thank Fires above and below), but I still refused to look him in the eyes.

"Brook?" the priest echoed. His tone changed – genuinely asking, or else just mocking. "Brook?" he repeated, feeling the name on his magyk-numbed tongue. I finally glared over my shoulder to keep him from saying it again. His thin mouth drew up in a smirk which didn't quite cover his face. His tongue ran over his teeth beneath his lips. The so-called stew of lentils and dried greens simmering on the fire suddenly looked even less appetizing.

"So that's what he called himself," he pondered. "Yes… it works. Good choice. Sounds like a Warden-name, at least. I wonder where he got it?"

For a moment, I thought he'd gone mad; I could make no other sense of what he said. Brook got his moniker from the order, from his captain – same as any other cadet. Even I knew that much about the Wardens.

Kirlinder's smile grew wider and no less sickening. The nameless acolyte busied himself with the pot, lifting the ladle to his lips to test the broth. His master raised a single finger, like a teacher giving a lesson. "You've been sorely used, my young friend," he said, making sure to put me in my place before he started – even if I'm only a few years younger than him. "We were tracking you when you met 'Brook,' as you call him. Making certain you were safe – you, and the prince," he added, tapping his bag. "But when we saw the company you'd fallen into, we knew we needed to act, and act quickly.

"Your companion was a Warden – once. A sheriff, as he likely claimed." I felt no need to correct him… not that he gave me the chance. "A sheriff. A sheriff from the north… with a face of crosshatch scars." He paused, looking into my eyes for some sign of recognition. There was none to find. He gave a patronizing chuckle. "You Gräzlanders really are a backwards bunch, aren't you?" His smugness slipped somewhat as he turned back towards the fire. "I thought everyone had heard the treachery of Sheriff Willow."

He didn't see my eyes light up. But I had heard it: another long, sad tale in a world which seems full of them, and another I didn't put down in my journal. And – though Kirlinder might not believe it – I heard the story from Brook himself. Willow, I suppose… if my kidnapper tells the truth. He told it to me on that night outside the Warden-shelter, as

Book II

the belt of stars wound overhead like a great silver serpent…

The look which just crossed my captor's tired face almost makes being kidnapped by him worth it. He must've seen me readying to indulge my vice and realized he'd be awake for hours more overseeing it. It's been a long day for the old man, after all: kidnapping and arson before breakfast, censorship after supper. Not that it's been short for me, either. Even if I felt impish enough to try and keep him awake, I'd be the one left snoring in the cold. Besides, there aren't enough pages in this thing for one of my stories… so much for a book of tales.

I don't even know why he's letting me write. He just shoved this book into my hands after supper, while the acolyte was putting up the tents. "I understand you write," he said, hardly looking me in the eye. "Write." He didn't need to say it twice.

Like his grand master in the city, he could hardly have imagined this old farmer would take to words like a fish to drink… or a farmer to drink, for that matter. ~~Arches~~, I could use a warm ale…

Come, sleep: bring dreams of better days. Waking's used up all my nightmares.

~the 'winter's fire' destroyed most private structures within shellingor before it was finally extinguished. the city was rebuilt into the purely military fortress it is today when the king's army arrived to reinforce the ælfali border~

II

Well… that didn't work.

I'd hoped a worldly, well traveled (sort of) farmer would have no trouble fooling a pair of milk-soft Capital priests. Seems my captors aren't so sheeplike as I imagined; my kidnapping should've made that obvious. Kirlinder reads with less patience than last night. This book's no longer a journal for my own thoughts and wonderings – he's made certain I know that. Its pages are for confession, penance… and learning. ~~Arches below~~, I'm back in the ~~damned~~ schoolroom.

My new teacher's fidgeting, and I remember the words of my old one: *Start at the start, end at the end.* I'll get to your "lesson" soon enough, father – for now, I'll write my "confession."

Three white tents on a cold white hill: that was our camp for the night, raised before this journal disappeared into Kirlinder's bag – couldn't have me writing unsupervised, after all. The acolyte had just finished his head-scratching work with the ropes and stakes, and was standing back to admire it. The tents looked like pavilions: each was larger than the one from my pack (the one I'd considered sharing with Brook), and was meant only for one. Individual quarters weren't something these priests were willing to sacrifice, even in the wilds.

Soon I found myself alone, bereft my usual companions (the prince and my journal) beneath a round roof of spotless linen. It didn't look like it could survive a good snowfall; just a week in the dirt would put an end to it. Not that I'm complaining: the thin fabric proved an unexpected aid. While the mage-fire burned (longer than I thought it could), I had a clear view of the figures next to it. The two gaunt priests chose to remain awake while I went to my borrowed bedroll with a half-faked excuse of exhaustion. They moved like shadow-puppets on the side of my tent as they held some secret conference beyond my hearing. Then one vanished: Kirlinder, I assumed, overdue for his elder's nap. That left only the nameless acolyte beside the fire.

I waited for him to retire as the last glimmers of strange pale firelight faded, then winked to naught. The boy hadn't moved. I listened for what felt an hour, but even on the windless hill alone for miles about, I heard nothing… though my ears are not so quick as they once were. He might still be out there.

Sleep didn't call so enticingly as I made it seem on these pages, as Kirlinder read over my shoulder. That didn't make it any easier to resist. I sat through two watches of the night at least – some of the longest I've ever endured, save those on the night that Jayceson was born. It had been a stormy eve, cruel as the one which poured its wrath out on Raligstae…

Kirlinder's wagging his finger now, ~~blast him~~ (oh, is that too strong a curse? ~~Go hang yourself from the lowest Arch~~). I guess he's right – my son's birth and the storm in the Barrows bear little on my confession. Still, I miss my old journal: no one ever told me what I couldn't write.

Upright on the bedroll (which I'd complain was cold, if it wasn't softer than half the beds I've slept on), my ears stretched long as a highborne ælf's for any sound: a tent flap opening, snow crunching underfoot, anything. Nothing came. The third hour poured into the fourth, and I felt sure he was abed… he had to be. Winding up my courage best I could, I crept forward, slid the knot between the flaps apart, and – with one last, deep breath – pulled it aside.

The acolyte was staring right at me.

Book II

The moon hung low above the dark line of the Guardians. The spires of Crowntop (yes, I named the hill: I had little else to do today) cut the pale light to ribbons, stretching shadows 'cross the mound. My tent was in the light, the one beside it in the shade, and the one beyond that was glowing 'neath the moon. The campfire, long exhausted, lay within the same bright beam as the acolyte hunched over its ashes.

A sensible man might've lowered the flap, crawled back inside his tent, and hoped the boy hadn't seen him. But I think I've proved myself unworthy of such a title already, and I was sure I'd moved too suddenly to go unnoticed, even in the half-light. He knew I was awake, and unless I wanted him to tell his master come morning, I needed to make it seem I had good reason. I stepped out of the tent, adding a groggy waver to my steps (which wasn't too difficult to fake) as I made my way towards one of the crown's stony points. I hoped I'd drunk enough to make my excuse for a midnight constitutional sound convincing. I made little urgent hops as I crunched along; anything to sell the illusion. It wasn't such a bad act, after all… and it might even have worked, had it needed to. As I drew as close as I dared to the acolyte, my useless ears finally caught something useful above the silence of the night: the quiet, nasal snoring of deep dreams. The boy was asleep!

I took a few more steps anyways. Was it a ruse? A trap? A test? Surely he couldn't have just dozed off in the open, not in that kind of cold. I paused; the drone changed neither pitch nor pace nor tone. The boy was asleep, alright – sitting up next to the ice-cold embers with his eyes half-open. Kirlinder must've told him to make sure the fire burned down properly… or to watch my tent. The old man failed to realize his disciple was as exhausted as he was, what with driving and cooking and setting tents all day. He must've dozed off before the flames gave up their last. What Fortune was this? Certainly not the capricious maid I've come to know on this journey.

So the boy was asleep. Good… but I hadn't thought past getting out of my tent undetected. All the planning I'd done was to lay out a ruse in my words: my only real weapon. My captors had a far better one… but I knew the acolyte didn't have a tablet in his necklace (it's broken, he claimed earlier, before desperately trying to close it back up). Kirlinder was asleep, and between the feats he'd done in Shellingor and the fire he'd lit on the hilltop, he'd probably exhausted his supply – probably.

Words weren't my only weapon, though. My mind wandered back to that night outside the Warden-shelter (sit down Kirlinder, I'll be brief). Brook, my only friend on the road (as I thought him then and think him now, ~~damn you~~) was licking the last of the roast foxhare off his fingers as I chewed on one of its legs. He turned to grab the ingenious crossbow which had earned our meal, examining the limbs for signs of wear before he wound them back. Between greasy mouthfuls, I marveled that such a powerful weapon could be so easily hidden. Brook, still possessing the spirit he had before the maze, sent a guffaw booming into the night. "'tisn't any wonder, farmer," he proclaimed, turning the bow in his hand for my examination. "You came from the Capital? Saw the civic's work?" As usual, question led answer; I only just nodded before he started again. "Trust me, those clever ~~sods~~ aren't half so sharp as our smithies – and not even in our tailors' league" (censoring a dead man's words now, Kirlinder? For shame). "Besides," he went on, scooting nearer, "it's not so hard to hide a weapon, if you know what you're about. ~~Arches~~, even you could do it" (you really are going for it, aren't you?).

Me? It was he who nodded a reply that time, as he crooked his leg and drew a glittering something from his boot…

That same knife appeared in my hand, glittering beneath a different sky as I kept one eye on the boy. *Don't hide it inside your boot*, Brook had explained, handing the blade to me hilt-first – *that's the key*. It's too easy to be separated from your boots, especially at night, when a hidden dagger would be the most useful. *Put it in your pants.* I laughed when he said that, but he glared, dead-serious. *Blade up*, he continued, *so you can grab the hilt.* He had a special-made sheath 'round his calf to hold the knife: I mimicked it with an old handkerchief.

My draw was not so smooth as Brook's: the wrapping came loose with the blade. I grimaced, then tossed it aside – but I was out of my tent, undetected, with a knife in my hand. Good. A good start, at least. Then...

Then, I had no idea. I'm a farmer, for Arch... for goodness' sake! Guile's no virtue for me – not one I teach my children, at any rate. What did I know of escaping captivity? My boots grew cold (and a trifle damp) as I stood with a bright silver blade in my hand and no thought in my head. If a cold breeze slipped through the wall 'round the hill and woke the acolyte, there'd be no convincing him I was just answering nature's call anymore.

Though perhaps I was. Nature, miles and leagues of it, empty in all directions, called out to me, but hope lay beyond the black horizons. If I ran (or started running, then fell to walking), I'd be a black dot on the spotless fields when the priests woke, and my tracks would lead them straight to me. I'd never reach Shellingor fast enough – tired and broken as the old mule was, he'd still be able to... the mule!

I looked towards the outskirts of the camp. He was taking a well deserved rest, same as everyone else (save me). Still muzzled needlessly, bit, bridle, and yoke sat heavy on his bended back: there were no trees nearby (not even dead ones), so the priests had left him hitched to the half-cart to keep him from wandering off.

Despite my lack of foresight, I must credit myself for some good thinking (I must be honest in my confessions, right?). I wasn't going to steal the whole cart. It would only slow me down, make me easier to follow, even if my tracks were only doubles of the ones we already made. I didn't know if the beast had ever been ridden. I knew I'd never ridden. Even so,

I liked my chances better on his back than at the reins, though my painful day in the back of the wagon might've swayed my choice.

The cart sat between two horns of the hill, beyond the campfire... just past the sleeping acolyte. I swallowed a cold hard dryness and gripped the knife tighter, ready to cut the harness loose and swing up into the non-existent saddle. With one more long look into the shadows on the youngster's face and one more long listen for any change in his breathing, I crept forward. The ice crunched beneath my boots (nearly soaked through by indecision), and I winced at every step. The drone of the disciple's rest wavered, but didn't change. I zig-zagged towards the cart, sometimes giving him the widest berth I could (moving towards the outer stones and circling 'round), sometimes moving straight for the cart (until I lost my nerve again). From above, my tracks must've looked like the edge of a key.

My heart beat a rhythm of *one two* four *three* as I passed the campfire (and it's ever-so-vigilant watchman), then began to catch itself on the downbeat: I was nearly there. I hurried, quiet as I could, towards the edge of camp. The fresh snow squeaked like a pack of rats. The acolyte kept sleeping; Kirlinder had worked him into a sleep I could not break. I oft wish to have the energy of youth again, but I forget it has its limits. Whenever Jayceson toppled into bed during the harvest, the Dome of Heaven could shatter and he'd still be halfway to the Dreamlands.

I glanced back to the cart – and froze. The mule's ears had twitched. Maybe it was some trick of the moonlight, I thought – then he turned his sleepy, lazy eyes towards me. They looked black as inkwells as they blinked out of his long, shaggy face. If recognition lit them, I didn't see it: I was backing away, both hands raised in a gesture of harmlessness as I prayed (blasphemous as it might be) he would turn away and close them once more.

My prayer went unanswered, if it was heard at all. The

muzzle hid the creature's brays beneath the cacophony in Shellingor, but in the windless, death-still night, his tired whinny cut the air like a knife. I spun 'round, knowing already what I'd see. The ears of the acolyte twitched as the mind between them woke. He stirred, snorted awake, and looked up – straight at the open flap of my tent. I didn't have time to kick myself then, but I am now. Half a second of thought would've saved me days of pain.

Sleep fell from his eyes when he saw it, glowing in the moonbeam and very, very empty. I had only moments before he raised an alarm, and I knew it. I just didn't know what to do to stop it. I'm not a man of arms; the Warden's knife, skillfully wrought, was awkward in my hand, feeling heavy as the sword I'd carried in the Barrow-maze. The only time I can remember striking someone (besides my many childhood brawls) was when I took that sleepy swing at the soldier in Northwall. But when the priest-in-waiting began to turn around, my placid nature fell away as one overpowering thought filled my mind. *Silence him!*

It wasn't so much a conscious thought as that. I didn't think to use my knife... I didn't think to do anything. My legs, arms, and hands were moving of their own accord before I could. The night grew hazy, my movements slow and clumsy and completely beyond my control – a feeling I knew all-too-well from my nightmares.

We were two steps apart when my feet left the earth. He had only the barest second to make sense of the sight: twelve-stone of blubber and grey hair with cloak flapping like a great brown wing behind. Then air and sense were knocked from us both as we rolled across the charcoaled leavings. ~~Thank Fires~~ the knife didn't go into the acolyte's belly (or mine). I don't know where it went – I hardly knew where my own thoughts were.

The boy's eyes stared back at me, wide and white as the hilltop as we rolled, one atop the other, then the other, through the ashes. Sleep hadn't fled from him – it had been thrown out at the first impact. Soot covered our hands and faces as we scraped and scrambled, and a fat black trail spread out behind us. If anyone was watching, they would've thought it funny: an old man wrestling a boy in the snow... if not for the knife.

I still held the ~~blasted~~ thing. It flashed back moonlight as we rolled in and out of shadow, sitting deadly in my undisciplined hand. Neither of us gave it – or anything else – a second thought. Deep down, I was fighting for my freedom. The boy was trying to keep it from me. But as we strained and grabbed and swung our fists (when we could get enough space to do it), we were no longer creatures of reason. Daggers are the tools of men, not beasts... but in the end, I had the misfortune to use it.

The boy and I tumbled away from the fire. I managed to kick loose as we rolled past Kirlinder's tent, landing clear of the desperate hands grabbing at my cloak. The acolyte rolled twice more before realizing I was gone. He turned and jumped up to one knee, staring back at me with ashes running from his saucer-eyes like black tears. His chest heaved in and out as he knelt, coiled like a spring. All his mind screamed for him to *Run! Run like mad!* I know mine did. Instead, he readied to jump.

Madness drove reason on unfamiliar courses. If I ran, I'd make it no further than the bottom of the hill – magyk or no magyk. Brook's dagger, like an unwanted finger, dangled from my hand as I clawed at the snow, kicking into the ice and charging on all fours – howling all the while. The wordless cry tore into the night as I pounced. I didn't look into a wash-basin today (obviously), but I'm sure my face is still streaked with ash like a war-painted Outerlier. The acolyte's eyes grew impossibly wider as he finally heeded the voice of his instincts.

That voice probably saved his life. I lashed out with my right hand as he tried to scramble away. The dreamlike slowness held: I watched the blade flash once in the moonlight before it cut deep into the boy's wide, bald brow just above his eyes. I don't know where my hand had meant to slash (it certainly didn't consult me), but I doubt it was there. Flesh parted. The knife, butcher-sharp but held by weaker hands than it was made for, skipped across bone and flew wide of its mark. The boy fell backwards, staring up at me for a long, disbelieving moment. Then blood poured hot and dark over his eyes, and he screamed.

I don't know what I planned to do next. That cry should've brought sympathy and terror at what I'd done. Instead, it brought only greater panic. Even without my mind, my body was still fighting to still that sound; the blade came back to my side, its keen point aimed at the boy. He was already clutching his forehead like a man with a headache, still screaming. One leg pushed through the snow as I leapt again.

I don't know what I planned. I didn't have to find out. A force like the one which nearly threw me to my death in the Barrow-maze hit me like a sparrow in a howlaround. The knife flew one way, my breath another, and I, unfortunate I, a third – clear over the destroyed firepit. The poor frightened mule brayed through its muzzle as my back met the snow and cut a new drift in the hilltop. I must've caught a breath mid-flight; air (and a bit of bile) exploded from my mouth.

The hillock darkened, though no clouds hid the moon. I laid unmoving, half-buried with all sensation far away and tingly. The boy's mouth was fixed open, his screams sounding as though they were miles distant. In the wide strip of darkness behind him, two brilliant, steely lights shone into the night.

Then I saw nothing. Nothing at all.

There were no dreams, good or ill, in that oblivion. Before all thought ceased, I wondered if this was the end: the unknowing unknowable of death before the Dreamlands. Then all was time: unmarked, and yet still felt, like the passage of a starless, moonless night. It was the best sleep I'd had in weeks.

What followed was less welcome. My senses returned from

their wanderings one by one: first sound, then (ow) feeling, then sight – the sight of a face the night had hidden. Kirlinder stared pensively against a sky too blue and cheery. He sat in the middle, with his boyish follower driving the mule to his left and me to his right, unceremoniously dumped into the corner of the wagon's seat. He'd been looking off over the horizon until I gave a loud, long-gestated groan: half from pain, half from anger and futility. He turned from contemplation, his smile either faked or full of sick delight. "G'morn, dear farmer," he cooed, sounding every bit the kindly village priest, "How do you feel?"

The way I sat did little to lessen the pain in my back, though they did drape a blanket (that same itchy quilt from yesterday) over my shoulders. Not that I allowed any gratitude to show. I slumped further into the corner (lighting my spine with fresh pain) and crossed my arms – then stopped. A peevish grin split my face. Yesterday, I'd laid a ruse of silent acceptance, useless as it proved. Time to make up for it.

The old man's face took the same flushed, blushed hue as his follower's as I loosed the stream; telling him how it felt to be taken prisoner by arsonists, bandits, and liars, thrown in the back of a wagon like so much unwanted produce, hauled halfway 'cross the wildlands, assaulted for trying to return home, and, worst of all, to know that my captors claimed some holy right to do it all. Kirlinder flinched at each accusation, his face turning further, to a sickly green. I didn't let up: I made clear (with words which left little room for interpretation) that he'd stolen the greatest task I'd ever been trusted with, slithering and sneaking and sabotaging when all he needed to do was ask. I'd have been happy to give him the prince. Instead, he put countless lives at risk, chief among them the man he framed (as I'm certain he did) to turn the city's eyes away from him.

The acolyte was near to glowing red; if he didn't need to hold the reins, he'd probably have covered his ears. I called words my weapon... the only weapon I have, now that Brook's dagger lies abandoned in the snow. With priests, it seems more than a metaphor. I couldn't help but feel proud: between a ragamuffing childhood on the streets of Halistoc and the long nights in roadside taverns since, I doubt any soldier, Warden, or fishmonger could swear so fine. I wonder... if I tried it again, could I make them both too ill to stop my escape?

Oh, he jumped at that. Think his face changed color, too.

Kirlinder's false smile was naught but a memory by the time I finished. Mine only grew wider until I ran out of words or breath or both. His eyes broke off as he turned back to the pale north Guardians. I sat back, slouching no more in my smug triumph. "I'm sorry you feel that way," he muttered, apology as disingenuous as my "confession" on these pages.

I settled back into the silence as hills rolled by around us. The sun had already climbed halfway up the sky and left most of the day wasted. Even so, the hours dragged by as the mule's rear-end bounced up and down in front of us. The cart moved heavy and slow with three men riding it and the drifts growing deeper than the wheels. The beast had finally been unmuzzled, probably as a reward for catching me. I'm glad my efforts earned somebody's freedom. Every once in a long while, the acolyte (whom I'll start calling Will if I don't get a real name soon... he looks like a Will) gave the reins a little tug to turn us 'round some steaming spring cutting through the snow. Besides that, our course ran true north. We're not headed for the Gräzland road: I know that for certain now, unless my captors are so lost they've forgotten which way the sun sets (which wouldn't surprise me). If anything, it seems we're headed for...

Kirlinder's waving me to finish. Once more, his sleep was cut short because of me. He knows I'm drawing to an end. All I have left to write is my lesson... my lesson, and one last confession: the day was unbearably dull.

Yesterday, I had something to do: namely, imagine the

horrors waiting at the end of the cart-ride. Today, I sat next to two holy men I would not (or could not) bring myself to speak to. Even if I had tried (I didn't), my paint-stripping outburst would've made them nervous to reply. If I had a journal, or even this pitiful excuse for a grammar book, I might've scratched down one or two of those unwritten tales; they returned to my mind again and again as I stared out at the dark horizon. Not that Kirlinder would've let me, even if he'd deigned to open his satchel. As we rolled into the earthwork ring circling a bone-white deadwood – our camp for the night – he made this notebook's purpose clear. He's given it to me for confession… and for learning holy writ.

Bah! Enough prelude, I guess. Kirlinder raised his voice just no: "Start your lesson, farmer," he said. And I will – soon as I make one more confession. This one is honest, I swear.

I hadn't noticed the linens around Will's head when I first woke – probably cut from one of the tents (probably mine). I didn't notice them until after I'd poured my wrath against Kirlinder into his burning ears. Once I did, I couldn't think of anything but the father in his hollow hill in Raligstae. Guilt, a total stranger to my mind, pulled at my quiet thoughts all day. I'm no Lost-One: I didn't mean to hurt him. I took no pleasure doing it. No – all my ill will is reserve for his master. Yet some part of me beyond my control or understanding did swing that knife. I don't recognize the wild man I just described; not even if he wore my face. ~~Arches~~, he hardly seemed like a man at all.

Well, at last you've forced me to it, Kirlinder. I've exhausted words, thoughts, and patience… yours, not mine. Besides, even if I slept for half the day, it waxes late, and I'm unearthly tired. So – your lesson.

I've hardly been inside a chapel since Obris fell asleep, and even when he was teaching me to read and write, he never let me soil the Book of Order with my grubby farmer's fingers. Kirlinder thought as much of me: he's quite sure I'm completely ignorant of all the great matters. When it comes to

Book II

scriptures, though, he's right as he can be. So we started with a hymn, not a story, even if it'd be easier to remember. I've never been much good with rhymes. He started humming it on the cart around the third hour of silence, when it became clear that no one else would break it. The melody was simple, lilting and familiar. Hymns all sound the same to me, which always made it easy to pretend I knew the words. He was midway through a second round when he turned and looked at me, a terrible inspiration in his eyes. Then he started singing; quietly at first, before Will picked up the chorus and their voices rose together. I tried not to listen; did everything short of sticking my fingers in my ears (I didn't want to give them the satisfaction). It didn't work. By day's end, they'd rounded those five stanzas at least two dozen times, and the words are now stuck in the wheels of my mind. Good thing, too: my lesson is to write them from memory. The ~~blasted~~ thing goes just so:

  Long ago in days o' darkest cold
  The shadows crept a'life
  Man cowed b'neath the midnight curse
  And fought in bitter'st strife.

                      The mothers wailed as children fell,
                      Black swords clutched in their hands
                      Blood poisoned all the wat'ring streams
                      And smoke drowned out the land.

  Yet hope remained in form divine;
  An unforesee'd right
  The gift which brought the glitt'ring day,
  The life, the sun, the light!

> Strength of Men! Stre – ngth o – f Men!
> Almighty Magyk stone!
> Grant kings of old with noble heads
> To reign from righteous throne!

Strength of Men! Stre – ngth o – f Men!
How wise they prove-ed be:
Divinity of forging Fires
In their bright ey – es see…

~readers may note the familiar character of the acolyte's wound. what few panopticon records remain have been consulted: the boy my father knew as will later became pontiff ægeas 'skarcrown' velicin~

III

My confessor has returned to me at last. After being separated from it last night by the clasping fingers of my tutor, I worried that he'd had all the could stand of my rudeness, crudeness, and imagined wit. Turns out he had – but only enough for one night. I'm much obliged, though the only confession I have today is that I have nothing to confess... nothing new, that is. Pray though, let me make some note of the day before I get to my lesson? Again, obliged. Maybe I'll even keep from swearing. No promises, though.

Our day began dark and ended darker. Accustomed as I'd grown to sleeping when I wanted and rising when I felt, I was none-too-pleased to feel the hand on my shoulder, shaking me awake before first light. After a week free from the Capital's sleep-after-sunset rise-before-sunrise schedule, I'm trapped in it again. They were far more cautious waking me than the city guard had been, for good reason. Groaning, I rolled over. Will knelt beside me. It's strange, but he always jumps back whenever I look at him (though it's not so strange now). A bloodied bandage was still wrapped around his forehead; given the way he'd earned it and my tendency to attack early morning visitors, he was wise to get some distance. If I hadn't felt a pang of guilt, I might've added a bloody nose to his injuries. I was barely conscious at that unearthly hour – my fist might've swung of its own accord again.

But the hour was hardly to blame. I oft think the morning hours are the finest in the day, though they usually don't start until after the cock's crow. No – for the first time since this mess began, my sleep was deep and free of nightmares. I fell asleep thinking of Jayceson, Senaia, and the uncomfortable knot of rope connecting my ankle to one of the pale trees outside; I woke thinking of the same. They were all more painful with the morning. My body must be greedy for rest, though – after so long a fast, one taste only made it hungrier.

For once, Kirlinder's the one keeping me awake, forcing me to write. Without him, I might've slipped off to bed without my nightly scribblings. Thank F… thank goodness our journey was much the same as yesterday's: there's little to record but its beginning and ending. That, and my teacher's tale.

Kirlinder made too much of my complaint about the hymn; I've leapt from lesson one to twenty. As we sat around the reignited mage-fire (he's not so short on stones as I thought) and bluntly broke our fast on bowls of lukewarm grits, my teacher began, without preface, to recite "The First Sequence of Progeneration." If ever I lifted the covers off the holy writ (galling as the thought may be) and read the first forbidden pages of that text, I imagine it's what I'd see. Or not: the writ has its own strange ordering, I'm told. Wherever it falls, it took most of the day to get it out, between endlessly repeating the tricky bits and answering the mostly insipid-questions pouring from my mouth.

He's not a bad teacher – even if he is a bad priest. Even so, he couldn't help growing more and more frustrated as the day rolled on. Either I was incapable of comprehending the scriptures, or I just couldn't convince myself to accept them without question, as he so clearly did. As we sat across the wagon bench, him speaking, Will listening, and me trying to learn, my teacher muttered to himself in the silence after each of my questions. At first I thought he was praying, but unless the private prayers of the elect consist of counting backwards from increasingly high numbers, I doubt it. When I made my last ask, just before the day wound down, his count was somewhere in the high hundreds.

Not that I was enjoying his lesson so much more (though I did enjoy Kirlinder's frustration). I'm grateful Obris suffered through long seasons of trying to teach me, but it's not as though I didn't suffer too. I never took pleasure in the lessons, just their fruit. Letters, words, and stories... those, I've always loved. Learning to read them... less so. It was always a means, long and winding. Obris would've pulled the hair from his head if he'd had any left. I've noticed Kirlinder's has started growing in, and not for want of a blade; Will's kept his scalp shining bright in spite of the bandage. I wonder how long it can last while he's teaching me.

It might've fallen out all on its own if I'd questioned him much longer. He'd only just finished the lesson for the first time (rounding back and starting over a dozen times) when the monotony of the wilds began to fail. Rounded hills, stretching east and west like great ripples in the earth, began to appear around us, climbing ever higher towards the mountains. As he began the story again (asking me to repeat it after him, line by line), Will put the reins (and then the switch) to the back of his faithful mule; he had difficulty believing the steep, slick rises were worth the climb. As I stumbled again over how to refer to holy Fires (as "they" rather than "he," it turns out), we cut switchbacks in the last fatted roll of the wide, white plain.

Kirlinder turned away suddenly (just as I was about to get it right), a look of wonder widening his dark, narrow eyes. The transformation was so complete, I had to see what caused it. My own eyes filled with the same astonishment: the horizon wasn't empty anymore. A deep black line cut its length like ink on virgin canvas. Still some leagues down the hill, a sheer obsidian wall rose out of the snow. It stretched out left and right beyond the range of sight, still standing a hundred feet or more (by my best guess) above the earth when it vanished.

A half-frozen river flowed across the plain from a mighty fissure in the rock, ragged as a knife wound. The stone, thank F... thank goodness, was not the same as the Barrows; it shone where the sun caught its sharpest edges, but the cliffside ate the light itself. I knew we only saw the foremost edge of that slab of Arch-glass. Beyond the horizons, it dove back beneath the Vale to the depths from whence it rose. I knew it as I knew the river marked the canyon which passed through its black heart; it was the Rift, after all. There's not a child of the north who doesn't dream about it.

It was a dream I let fade, and I confess I never saw it until today. I'd always said I wanted to make the journey: first to my ne'er-do-well friends in Halistoc, then to Senaia, across warm pillows on our first winter nights together (goodness, I think Kirlinder just blushed). But then came Jayceson, and all the work of fatherhood. Childhood dreams seem silly beside such cares. Even when I started making the Autumnal trek with my boy, we always left too late to make the detour and returned too tired to walk the extra leagues. Once or twice, we spotted its edge from the crest of some high hill; Jayceson would point, and I'd turn away with a pang of regret. Congratulations Kirlinder, you've made my dreams come true... nightmares included.

In spite of that longing, I wasn't so happy to see it as I might've been – oh, stuck dumb for sure (much to the relief of my tutor), but as we passed over the last bit of flatland and the wall loomed heavier and heavier overhead, dread as cold as the snow on Crowntop poured down my back. The reason for our odd course was growing clearer. Once we passed between those dark slabs taller than any castle wall, no watching eye would be able to espy us – captor, cart, or prisoner. As that gaping maw yawned wider before us and any chance we might turn away grew smaller, I noticed (despite Kirlinder loudly resuming his lesson) that the teeth were not so dark as they first seemed: glimmering orange points shone from deep within the dark of days. *Hungering eyes*, I thought to no one but myself. The lights grew in number as the fissure folded 'round us, and the light of the already fading sun disappeared. It wasn't nightfall; I turned and saw the bright snow and sky glowing between the walls at our back.

Kirlinder was trying to keep me distracted. It wasn't working. For the fourth time in as many minutes, I asked him to repeat himself. His voice rose, urgent and obvious in its effort to turn my attention from the flames gathering 'round us. Poor Kirlinder... Brook knew the secret to distracting me from fear was to let me do the tale-telling. Instead, he wasted breath while I watched the torches close in like willow-wisps to a lamp. They stopped some ten feet from the cart, leaving a clear path for our animal. Assembled, their torches cast barely enough light to see them. Their hoods and cloaks looked darker than they had in the market, but I had no trouble recognizing them for the Capital's priests – not this time, at least

My young friend was spared from raising camp; the other clergymen had already set their tents (and three empty ones) along the ribbon of the snowmelt river beyond the first bend of the canyon. By their numbers, it seems half the order is camped here, in a spot not half so pleasant as our last two camps. The unnatural dark lay heavy over all we did. A hairline crack was all that remained of the sky throughout the day, but even that's gone dark now (thought I think I see the starry band, cutting through the black above). It's the closeness that makes it so unbearable; I can think of no other word for it. The chasm feels even narrower than it is, and the dizzying height of the walls makes the idea that it's stood for a thousand years laughable. It's not just the walls which feel closed in: the air itself presses down on us, thick as when it choked me in my bed at Shellingor – not quite strangling, but just short of it. There's a magyk here, and I knew it soon as we entered, a dark beyond the art of torches to drive back. All their light can do is cast twisted images in the walls, like long-dead visions of the Dark-Days.

I pray to whatever power hears ones such as I that we don't tarry here. I doubt we will: the Rift stands on the Ælfali border, running a short ways north to where it rises at the river's source, just below the Firns. Oh yes, teacher, I do know some things; though my feet led me far west of the stone, I studied it as best I could when I was still a boy. If our course is still half-sensible (I have my doubts), we'll be out of the canyon and at the feet of the cliffs in a few days. I've given up my dreams of escape. Much as I loathe the present company (the new priests have done me no harm, but I'm sure they're just waiting for Kirlinder's word), my part will be over sooner if I just obey... though I still wonder at their conduct. Kidnapping, burning, looting, and binding, before starting me in on a study of scripture.

And speaking of which... I may as well begin. Again, I'm out of words (hard as it is to believe). I'll let Kirlinder take over.

"In the age long past, in the void before the Vale, two almighty Fires burned against the dark," he began, his breakfast balanced on one knee. "There was naught but the two Fires: no light, no heat, no thought beyond their own. For the Fires were living, thinking things; blazing with intent and insight beyond any mortal mind. But burning greater still was all their hate for one another. For one was the Fire of Order, that power which holds all things together and binds creation in perfect unity, while the other was the Fire of Chaos, making all things grow and change and fall apiece in time. Locked in enmity..."

Kirlinder stumbled; I squeaked out my first question. *How could fires burn, with nothing to burn?* I asked. The answer came soon as Kirlinder's count (only from ten this early in his lesson) had finished: I was sitting beside the solution, after all. With all the mage-fire I've seen in the last few days, I should've known not every blaze needs match or tinder. The fires I knew, Kirlinder expanded, were but shaded reflections and poor copies – even his own magyked ones. To be honest, the answer felt somehow thin... but I hardly wanted another withering glare from Kirlinder. Or from Will, for that matter: his opinion of my ignorance was plain as the milk dribbling down his chin.

"Locked in enmity for all of endless time, the Fires strove in power, one against the other, in wars which shook the infinite. But neither could claim a victory, for burning ever brighter and hotter, they only added to the other's light and heat. This they knew, and feared, and fell away... but ever they glimpsed the other's glory, until instinct drove their flames against each other in an endless cycle. At the end of ages, both burned so blinding bright that the bounds of naught could no longer hide them. In one fierce and final battle, they met, and blazed, and tried to flee, but their burnings were so vast that there was no dark left to conceal them. And so they burned, trapped – unable to fight. Rather, they looked, and, for the first time in all the eons... they drew close in curiosity.

"Both flared brighter than e'er before, yet for once, they desired no destruction. Each saw in the other what they'd missed before: the strange, alien beauty of their foe and the foul darkness of the void. From bound to bound they burned, feeling, searching for what might be found and finding nothing."

How Fires felt anything, I had no idea. As our cart rolled out from the earthen gate of the mound, I thought to ask, but withheld. *Answers will come*, I assumed – but they didn't. Still haven't. But Kirlinder's no more in a mood to teach than I am to learn. Some other day, then.

"The emptiness displeased them both. The Fire of Order saw fruitless dark and desired systems in the blackness to shape and structure all that was. The Fire of Wrath saw perfect, eternal simplicity and desired all things begin and end and begin again. Neither could abide, yet neither could make perfect their vision, for bright as they burned, the void was colder still. And so, seeing in their enemy all that they lacked, they enjoined, and partook both light and heat and behold! The Fire of Creation, bright and true, swept aside the dark. The void dissolved in flame, and thence came land and air and sky and sea, and when the Fire reached the bounds of all that was, they turned back upon the newborn Vale."

I wanted to stop him again (really, I did), but we were just crossing the doorstep of the Rift when he reached this part the second time, and more mundane fires were distracting me from his speech. Still, his talk of holy Fires was utter nonsense…

Sorry, it seems I was wrong – half wrong. I may not be in the mood for learning, but Kirlinder still has some lessons in him. At least he didn't snatch the book out of my hands this time.

"Nonsense?" he started, rising to his feet. The other priests jumped at the sudden noise. He shrank slightly, then sat back down. "No, gräzlander, not nonsense – high truth. The very good." He chuckled to himself. I'm sure he felt his condescension justified; the answer was right there in front of me again.

"Look," he said, pointing to the cookfire, "see the lines of ember there: the patterns, glowing in the dark. See them?" I nodded – even in the sallow mage-fire, the logs, cut and carried from our last camp, had burned down to husks which glimmered from within. "Were they there before? Hiding somewhere in the logs?" He didn't wait for an answer (I thought they might've been) before chuckling again. "Of course not. But by burning what was there – wood, sap, bark – the fire made something new. Something beautiful." He turned back. I didn't much like the look in his eyes as he stared into the dying fire.

Hours before in the seat of the cart, his story went on without interruption. "Long did the Fires burn at the edges of the Vale, beneath Heaven's darkened Dome. Their light encircled all, illuminating what their union made. Each saw their desires made manifest – yet also the desires of their foe. For the Flames of Order and Chaos burned together, but they could not be united. As they blazed above the mighty mountains, their tongues lashed against one another, arguing within.

"Order saw unmoving earth and the strong Arches below, yet also the lapping water cutting channels in the ground. Chaos saw wild, free winds and the roiling skies, yet also the mountains which would stand for all the ages. The Fires had been deceived.

"Long they burned in fury, a mere shadow of their ancient wars; yet their hate was hot enough to blast the sands beyond the Guardians to glass, birthing the dead Outerlies. Order wished to form moving things upon the ground, to turn aside the changes Chaos wrought. Chaos, for a time, wished to rejoin with Order to become the Fire of Destruction, burning away what they had made to make it anew, and on and on unto eternity. But neither could be satisfied, and their hate became too terrible to endure.

"They fled in anger, scattering to tongues which dove and swooped above the Vale. But escape came at a cost: for even in the dark of the sunless sky, all the land divided the disperate flames, small and lost and too dim for sight. As Order fled the sparks of Chaos and Chaos the flames of Order, they flew across the valley's face, searching for the great Fires which gave them birth. But those Fires were gone, splintered to a hundred thousand candle flames, ancient minds lost in a burst of glowing embers.

"Long they sought in vain, 'til light and hope were almost lost. Alone in a dark world which dwarfed its makers, the remnants of Creation's Fire burned out one by one – slowing, stopping, then falling to the frigid earth.

"Then came the greatest wonder – for as the Fires smoldered in the dust, the ground itself leapt sudden to flame and smoke, and from it sprang strange, moving things: bird and beast and branch and bough. Where the sparks of Order and Chaos met, too wearied to fight… mankind stood, rising to divine life in an instant.

"And thus," said Kirlinder, drawing his tale to a close, "begins the Progeneration: the beginnings of all within the Vale." He sat back in his seat; had he been reading from a book, I'm sure he would've clapped it shut. A fondish smile broke his thin, harsh face. "This is holy writ," my tutor intoned, unknowingly repeating the very words I'd heard not-so-long ago; "This is the very good. Know it – and be at peace."

My blood ran cold at the reminder of Raligstae… or would've, had I not the overwhelming urge to laugh.

This is holy writ? Once and half again over as ludicrous as any legend I've ever heard? That forbidden book, unopened in every chapel I've ever wandered into, always gave me a rush of reverent fear. Had I known it was a book of færie-stories…

Fine! Yes, that's going a bit too far, even for me. Kirlinder certainly thinks so: I just spent the last five minutes arguing with him to let me finish. I meant no disrespect (well, maybe a little), but I can recognize (and fear) those things which lie beyond my comprehension. There's much I don't understand: this journey's shown me nothing if not that. Secondvessels, World-Serpents, Earth-Piercers, death-dances… I still understand little and less of what they all mean. Even so…

Fires that don't need wood, making the world in a moment by burning nothing? Men made of smoke and women born of earth? Just read those words as *I* write them, Kirlinder, and tell me they aren't the sort of thing one tells a child. Your holy writ could be true: if such a thing happened, it was long before anyone could remember. But believing it without proof? That's putting a muzzle on everything I do know… a better one than you put on the mule.

Book II

Is this what priests call faith? If so... well, simpleton children must be the most faithful creatures around.

~my father's knowledge of the rift's geography was quite exact. his knowledge of the vale's politics was not. the rift was and is a territory of the sovereign realm of œlfal~

The Gräzland Tales

Book II

VI

This morning, I woke to cold, dark, and screaming in the Rift. My eyes forgot sleep as the high howl of pain and panic cut through my tent, and I nearly forgot my nightmares – returned now, after two nights of peace. Only fitting they return in this evil place... and yes, Kirlinder, I really do believe it's evil. Perhaps just as evil as Raligstae, with waking terrors to match the sleeping ones.

I lay motionless, wanting to scream as well but unable to: the all-too-familiar paralysis of dream's end froze my lungs. At first, I thought Kirlinder's sapping spell (punishment for my irreverence) hadn't faded with the night, and whoever (or whatever) was attacking the camp would find me as soon as it was done with the priests. I imagined the tent flap pulling back and a terrible face (one of the twisted reflections from the cliff walls) looking down at me with a wolfish grin...

The echoing screams changed character as sleep drifted away... though that's not really true. I just heard them for what they were: winding and thin and too high for a human. Not even an ælf could reach that pitch. As my frozen joints thawed one by one, I rose from the mat with a creaking groan.

I stepped out of my tent (retrieved from the wagon the new priests brought, spotless white and never used) to a sight I welcomed no more than my nightmares. The night had not rolled back: I saw a scar of frozen lightning in the darkness where the dawn should have glowed, but no sunrise shone upon our camp. What light met my eyes was dull and red and stinging, as my sleep-tender eyes blinked against the smoke. The cookfire had been rebuilt as a bonfire, scratching at the dark with long red fingers and sending tall, gaunt shadows dancing on the walls like spokes on an axle of flame. The priests huddled 'round the firepit, swaying and murmuring. Their shadows leapt and twisted like the Lost-Ones in the death-dance. Between sunless dawn, fire, and holy histories rolling through my head, I felt like I was staring through a picture-window on the Dark Days. A new terror grabbed me as I watched: were the priests undertaking that black rite? Had the darkness of the Rift turned them to such foul magyk? And what, ~~by Heaven's Dome~~, was that terrible screaming?

The answer came flying at me like cork from bottle, fleeing the ring of priests. It was pink, fine-furred, and no larger than a bread pan, but it was fast; too fast for the priests, who stopped chanting and started giving chase, tripping on their own cloaks and the cloaks of their neighbors. The creature's tiny hooves beat the stone as it slipped out of their clumsy, grasping hands. One managed to snatch its coiled tail, nearly holding on before it slipped from his fingers and bolted for the canyon's exit – straight towards me. I realized why the squeal had sounded so familiar: I'd heard it oft enough in Ellingston, between the butcher's shop and the fields of the Gräzland games…

The festival. It was that memory which got me moving. Every year before the harvests of my almost-forgotten youth, I'd been the champion for little Ellingston; and quite the champion at that, with Senaia's scarf 'round my arm to wake my meager courage. The priest's wayward piglet was quite a bit smaller than the game pigs (and I quite a bit older), but I doubted it had been greased. If I could just remember how to time it...

I turned right, making to grab. The squalling runt turned left, failing to notice my legs still pointed that way. Just before it reached me, I fell sideways (a more painful maneuver than I remembered), wrapping my arms 'round its belly. Tiny cloven feet wheeled for purchase, but it couldn't escape my grip: a life behind the plow does give some good gifts, besides rheumatism.

The pig screamed louder than ever as two hooded holy men rushed over, plucking the pitiable creature from my arms without a word of thanks – or any word at all. They carried it back towards the fire by its hind legs, each held in both hands by both priests. I barely resisted the temptation to call out *Y'welcome* as I rose, brushing dirt off my already-soiled clothes. I've worn them day and night for two weeks now; they must reek of half the Vale. Not that I could smell them: my senses were dulled and dazed by sleep and shock and the sideways tumble. My skull rang like a bell. The screams had been nigh-unbearable when I'd been sheltered in my tent. The piglet screaming in my face as I held it steady was several dozen times worse. My ears were singing, my eyes were rimmed with dreamseed, and my body felt apt to tear itself down the middle for pain. I took a long stretch to try and fix all three. No luck. Yet as I watched the priests step aside to let the pig and its handlers through, I forgot all those complaints.

Kirlinder stood with his back to the fire, a terrible shadow. The white of his eyes, teeth, and spotless stole shone out of the red... as did the knife. My knife. Brook's knife. I recognized it before I recognized who was holding it. It glittered in the firelight like it had in the moonlight, when I'd last held it on Crowntop. I was sure it had been left behind, buried in the snow 'til Brightthaw, but there it was: a short Warden's blade, held point-down in the hands of a priest.

The dæmon shadows on the cliffs stood still, leaping now and again with the fire. Will stood at Kirlinder's side, the sight of the all-too-familiar blade chilling his blood (though I couldn't quite tell if he was really any paler than usual). His wound had been unwrapped; to let it breathe or to show reverence, I still wonder. A dark, jagged line bisected his brow. Pity welled at the sight… with no small measure of guilt. Although, come to think of it, it might make an attractive scar. It would do him little good if it did; he's sworn everything (body included) to the church.

Kirlinder, the pig, and its handlers soon had my attention back. The beast kicked desperately for the drop to freedom as it reached the front of the crowd. Kirlinder's narrow eyes, glowing blue against the fiery shadows, looked the animal up and down. I'm not sure where it came from, but it's not as though the priests could've caught a wild piglet in the Rift. There were a few crates in the wagon, I saw: one or two had holes for air.

Kirlinder nodded. With one last monumental effort (monumental for soft-limbed city-folk), they lifted the writhing animal above their heads. I thought sure their grip on its sausage legs would fail; it bounced and writhed, sensing its fate but unable to change it. The knife rose in Kirlinder's spiderish hands, gleamed against the fire, and then…

Sorry, but it seems a confession must interrupt my confession. I was just caught writing without permission; wasting invaluable sheets of cheap paper on words which didn't come from Kirlinder's mouth. Tale-telling… as always, a vice and vixen. But when Kirlinder pulled my little red book from his bag and left it on one of the stones by the campfire, the young ruffian from Felliswell (or Halistoc, that is) took hold. I learned quick fingers (and quicker feet) in those days. Taking my journal and a torch borrowed from the edge of camp, I made an excuse (the same as I meant to use in my failed escape) and snuck off.

Yes yes, I'll get back to it, teacher. ~~Arches~~, these priests are unbending as the cliffs... though he is letting me finish my tale. It bears on his lesson, after all.

I blinked. Alright, fine: I shut my eyes. The squealing cut short. When I opened them again, the deed was done: the piglet hung unmoving. Kirlinder held the knife to one side, a look of ecstasy on his pallid face. His eyes rose to the sliver of fiery sunrise heaven above, his mouth drawn tight in a cloying smile. His lips barely parted as he whispered three words just loud enough to hear: "Remember her mercies."

I thought those were his words, at least. My uncertainty vanished as every voice (save mine) took up the phrase. The Rift roared, mantra rebounding from the stones. And my ears had only just stopped ringing, too. The rite completed, the priests holding the lifeless animal carried it 'round the fire to the long spit waiting there. A few more moved to help, or else gathered nearer to the sizzling, popping spectacle. It was time to break the fast.

Don't think me ungrateful: after days of flavorless Panopticon porridge, fresh bacon was like a pint of golden ale. I just had difficulty convincing myself to eat it at all. Something about the butchering felt off-kilter, and it wasn't just Kirlinder using a Warden-weapon. That seemed sacrilegious all on its own (if the order can be called religious), but add to that the stomach-turning memories of Crowntop it recalled... not to mention memories of Brook...

I pray he's all right – the only real prayer I've uttered in years. What Kirlinder says about him can't be true, not after how he tried to help the people of Raligstae, not after how he tried to help me...

It hardly mattered at breakfast, but even so, it kept my stomach from righting itself as Kirlinder watched me from across the bonfire (burned down to a sensible cookfire by then). I tried to raise the salted pork to my lips, tasted gall, and set it back down again – and again – and again. Kirlinder chuckled; never a welcome sound. "It's only pork, farmer," he said, waving his last bite (twice the size of my share) before he inhaled it. "It doesn't disagree with you, does it?" For once, his question, got out between bites, seemed genuine.

It did disagree with me, I wanted to say – just not with my stomach. Instead, I spat out that I had no trouble with the food, punctuating my point with an overzealous bite. I only managed it by not actually looking at it or thinking about it… but it did taste heavenly.

Kirlinder took my meaning, and some of the smugness drained from his face, though his smirk remained. "No, I guess you wouldn't," he said, nodding as the flames cast vexing shadows up the stony sides of his face, "I forgot the sacrifice isn't practiced up north. Shame." He shook his head, then added: "I'm glad you got to see it here, though."

I nearly spat up the remains of my bacon (the taste of which gave my stomach final say over my mind after the first bite). *Glad?* How could he be glad in any way about that horrible, bloody rite? Where I come from (backwards as it might be), butchers don't take pleasure in the slaughter… nor trick others into helping them do it!

I told him so, though not in words so few or kind. Kirlinder (and more than a few of his fellows) took the sickly pallor which so oft follows my words. Yet behind that pale redgreen color, his face twisted with deep hurt… an expression I never expected to see on him. "No no," he began, so flustered that it shook me, "that's not what I…" His lips pressed together as he breathed through his nostrils, then started over. "I didn't take pleasure in killing that poor creature. By Heaven's Dome, I pitied it." I found that doubtful (and even more so now), but in the moment, I could've sworn tears were swimming in the corners of his eyes. "I held no more malice towards it than any butcher would. No more than you did, when you caught it." I turned, glaring down into the bowl holding my even-less-appetizing second course. I hardly needed the reminder. "But man needs meat," he carried on, "and – even more so – they need sacrifice."

He said it so earnestly, so matter-of-course, that it took me a moment to realize he was talking nonsense again. My eyes turned up, confusion dancing behind. It must've looked amusing; Kirlinder chuckled to himself again. "I believe," he said once the laughing fit had passed, "I've found your next lesson, farmer."

Hours later, as our classroom rolled further and further into the dark, he made good on his threat. Camp was struck as the last breakfasters heaped their dishes in the cook's bag; the mage-fire winked out with a word. The long-handled torches around the camp stayed lit and left as we did, carried by the priests or else mounted to holsters on each wagon. The passing hours brought no more light into the canyon, except a little near midday. The nightmare glow of the torches followed us as our wheels rumbled over the stones.

Kirlinder's lackies arrayed themselves between the supply wagon and our oh-so-familiar half-cart. We rode near the front, behind two silent priests who lit the hard, uneven road ahead. The rest of the priests and the covered wagon hauling our food, tents, and ~~maj~~ followed, with two more cloaks trailing behind as rear-guard. I rarely saw them. Our poor old mule (whom I've taken to calling Phil – get it? Will and... oh, never mind) clopped along as Kirlinder began the second in what threatens to be an endless string of lessons. I'd seen Phil palling about with the other mules last night: broken, shaggy messes of grey and black hair that look almost like his kin. They probably are. The Capital's pool of livestock is shallow as its sea is deep.

Will listened in as Kirlinder spoke, a new, unsoiled bandage wrapped around his already mending wound. He only heeded the reins at a few tricky bends in the river. The story transfixed him; it should've transfixed me. Instead, I spent the day glancing up at the line of blue above, trying to remember that the waking world persists outside this dark land of memory and magyk. I felt like an ant trapped between two pavers: alone, and very, very small.

Yes yes, Kirlinder, I'm getting to it, stop waving your ~~damned~~ hand around. ~~Arches,~~ but city-folk are impatient. His tale seemed to follow the last, if his book is strung together sensibly. At least this one takes place in the world I recognize, if only just: Vale instead of void, and men and women in place of Fires... even if they act just as strange. Kirlinder's been peculiarly insistent about his words, making me repeat them several times after him. I kept my questions few. We covered more ground today than yesterday – in the story, that is. Our passage slowed as the canyon walls grew narrow, but my teacher hardly noticed; he was able to repeat his whole tale three times over before the fissure of light darkened, signalling day's end.

"In the first days, there was a great confusion amongst all living things," he began. There was great confusion in me too; I had to keep from asking if the first days weren't the ones in his last story. "Men and women," he continued, "born sudden of earth and char and great minds long lost, rose upon the face of the great wide Vale, scattered and knowing not from whence they came. Order and Chaos blazed within their bones, united – but not one.

"Their conflict blackened the hearts of men, and where they met, blood ran down in rivers; for they knew not what sort of creature stood before them... only the hatred of those ancient foes. And so they fought, and killed, and died in vain. One lived longer than most, triumphing bloody over all she met.

Book II

Broken bodies lay along her path, and whispers of *the Dead-Maker* arose behind her. For she was wise in battle, firm in limb, and keen of ear and thought – but even so, she knew not what she was. The flames which gave her birth raged, and threatened to tear her asunder.

"That was, until, on the day which Fate ordained, the Dead-Maker rose from her bed of polished stone to wander north across the Vale. Coming to a wide, clear pool in a black and burned plain, she knelt to drink, weary and thirsty from her long journeying. The pool sat below the burning mountain, whose light was hidden by the rising smoke. As she knelt beside the water's edge, all wind in the wide Vale ceased, and in the dark Heavens, still dimmed in the days before the sun, a single star shone forth in dazzling brilliance. It glimmered but a moment in the deepest dark, but in that moment the Dead-Maker faced a mirror smooth as crystal-glass. Within it, she saw a face not so unlike the faces of her prey.

"She raised her fists to strike; the image did the same. She recoiled, but her reflection fell back as well. Knowledge too terrible for thought began to dawn as the star above faded: her prey had not been monstrous beasts – but creatures like herself."

Or the Dead-Maker was the monster. The thought crossed my mind, but not my lips. Good thing, too: Kirlinder's writing *murder* with his eyes now. If he can master Brook's trick, maybe I should learn as well. It seems a useful skill.

My teacher (much friendlier looking as he sat beside me on the wagon) went on uninterrupted... in his first telling, at least. When he got to that odd star a second time, I had to ask where it came from. Chuckling, he set a finger along his nose like a man with a secret (a gesture my uncle was fond of using). "Don't be greedy now," he said, "That's another story, for another day." Uncle Illin used to say that too... though I don't know how many more days he expects to have; at this

53

rate, it'll take a year to get through the whole book.

"The Dead-Maker," Kirlinder continued (with a quick count down from ten), "fled screaming, eyes opened to the truth, thirst forgotten in mindless terror at all she'd done. But she was not alone upon that blasted plain. Far off, a lone man gazed in wonder at the sudden splendor of the starbeam before it faded back to dark. He drew near in curiosity. The screams of the Open-Eyed One echoed from the mountains, and every nerve and sinew in his body called to him: hunt, chase, kill or be killed. As ever before, he obeyed.

"Even blind with fear, the eyes of the once-called Dead-Maker saw his shadow in the long dusk. Unable to kill another foe (for it'd be as though she destroyed herself), she turned and fled up the fiery mountain towards the ever-rising smoke. The man gave chase, lagging only paces behind as stone and ash fell away beneath her feet. By the choked light of Arches' fire, she saw her own face staring back out of another's. Faster still she ran; but she could only run so far. Climbing over the blasted precipice, the Open-Eyed One saw she was trapped betwixt molten flame and a killer she could not kill. Turning back as her pursuer scrambled over the last ridge, she considered for a moment the end which fire could make. But she would not destroy herself, and so she turned to fight. She would not kill, but neither would she die.

"Long they strove in the sickly light, two dark shapes atop a dark hill. Blow for blow the Open-Eyed One, the once-called Dead-Maker, met her terrible foe. Hours turned to days as they wrestled in the choking soot; one for life, one for death. Both grew gaunt and dry as bone, choked by the earth-furnace at their backs. Wonder grew in the killer's mind at what manner of creature he faced, for none had ever fought so long or so well. And yet that admiration did not slake his blood-lust. Every Fire burning within him demanded death.

"Many times the Open-Eyed One might've struck a killing

blow, and many times she was tempted. Yet even in the twisted light, she saw her very face looking back upon her, and so fought on with all her skill and strength to keep them both alive.

"But even she would fall, for all warriors succumb to time. As the seventh day passed and the Open-Eyed One felt their limbs grow wan and weak, she considered again the lake of fire. But then her enemy buckled at the knees and collapsed, unmoving, to the earth. The Open-Eyed One, no more than skin-stitched bones, fell too.

"She had won. Both she and her foe still drew breath. And yet his breath was thin and choked, as dry as the ash. If he rose again, he would not survive the climb down the mountain's treacherous face. Rising slowly, unsure herself if she could make the journey, she realized what she must do.

"The man did not rise that day; the young Fires within him knit his broken body together as he slept. Sunless day and moonless night passed by before he stirred. His eyes opened; the Open-Eyed One stood with her foot upon his chest, a large, flat stone in her hands. The mighty man whimpered, trying to flee, but his arms had not the strength to scramble away, nor his legs to stand. The killer fell flat and waited death.

"But it did not come. The stone did not come crashing down upon his head. Instead, the Open-Eyed One knelt, and held it out to him. The man saw it was hollow, filled with pure, clear water from the mirroring pool below. Long he stared up at the offering, Fires striving against his thirst. Finally, wondering if she meant to poison him, he took the bowl and drew it to his lips. As he did, the mountain leapt with fire, and blood-red light spilled across his face. In the smooth surface of the water, he saw what the Open-Eyed One had seen, and screamed – but only for a moment. For the Fires within him flickered with a changing wind, and he realized the one before him was not an enemy.

"He drank deep the waters of knowledge, and when his thirst was sated, he stood beside the Life-Maker, looking out upon the Vale. By the light of the mountain, they saw the lost and scattered children of Creation fighting and killing and dying fruitless. The Flame of blessed Order rose at the sight against accursed Chaos, defeating it at last, and in that moment, they two became the first king and queen of the Vale; the Fire of Order, divinity incarnate."

I know the royals claim as much… ~~Arches~~, I was even angry when that student implied they weren't. Still, after seeing old Grett stooping in his throne and barely able to stand, I'm beginning to have my doubts. Yes, I know it's blasphemous, Kirlinder – stop making the form! Do you want me to think about these lessons or not?

The story picked up speed as our wagon came to a halt. A crack in the stony floor put an axle-breaking drop in the road, and the priests spent half an hour prying boards off the side of the wagon to make a ramp. Will, wanting more than anything to keep listening, jumped down to help them. "Living together in peace, they learned much of one another," Kirlinder droned on. "They learned how they could share their intelligences, born of once-united Flames, and so spoke the first words of ancient Valeian. Together, they learned to kindle fires, like but lesser than the ones which gave them birth, to cast the dark and cold aside. What's more, they kindled a yet greater fire; for they discovered their power to bring life from lifelessness by their enjoining as man and woman. Soon, they swelled to a mighty clan, sons and daughters of purest Fires born to save the Vale."

I squelched my doubts again. Discovering… well, *that* – makes sense. What comes more naturally? But inventing their own language? Even if they loved words half as much as I… come now, you have to admit that's strange. Is it impossible?

Book II

No... just like mythic Fires aren't impossible. Just unlikely.

"Yet even so, the Firstking and Queen lived no easy life. For the fires they lit drew many and more to their camps. As the Firstking had chased the light of the first star, so too did all men see them and grow enraged at the sight of Order's flame. But the Firstking was strong, and the Life-Maker valiant, and together they defeated every foe, casting them down and making them look upon the waters of knowledge. Many they were who turned and joined them, but many and more refused. The fire of Chaos burned fierce in mankind's heart, too fierce for Order to curtail. Knowledge only made hate grow, and the Open-Eyed One, unable to kill, carried her prisoners far into the wilds and there left them, alive and filled with rage. Greater and greater the royal clan grew, yet more numerous and fierce their enemies became. War-bands bound together to snuff out the Flame, and Chaos-borne they attacked the holy tribe year after year, killing those who would not kill.

"For a time they endured, weeping to see that men could not change; not even when faced with themselves. But the tears for their slaughtered children, brothers, and sisters wore down their pity, and the slain grew too many to count. At last they could remain no longer in the world of blood and dark, trying to save the unsaveable. From the precipice of the fiery mountain so many years ago, the King-Father had beheld a beauteous island, sheltered in a wide clear sea. As the slaughter grew unbearable, he chose, in secret, to find a way across the treacherous waters. Alone, he hulled the last of the great and ancient oaks to build the Vale's first ships, a fleet to carry his people to safety" (Quite the shipwright, this Firstking).

"When her children's blood at last became too high a price for peace, the Firstking revealed his works to the Life-Maker and begged her let them flee. Long she'd struggled, hoping for some way to save the hateful tribes, but even her great mind had failed to find it.

"They crossed the sea by dark, she and her King and all their many children, landing safe upon the isle's wide banks. Stepping from the boat, she turned back to where the hungering eyes of hate stared after her from the far shore. In a loud voice, she cried that all who rejected peace were forsaken, naming them as Outerliers: creatures of Chaos and wrath. Never more would she give her children's lives to save their thankless hearts.

"But peace was not to last," Kirlinder continued, spoiling my hope that the story might end with a *happ'ly evermore, unto the fading of the sun*. "The hateful Outerliers gathered in the wastelands, Chaos burning hotter still to see the light of Order bright and free across the night-dark sea. Many tried to cross its waters and extinguish it, but all fell, drowning in the unyielding black." I shuddered, remembering my own passage across those waters; harrowing enough, even with a bridge. Had I known the seabed was littered with the bones of ancient warriors… ~~Arches~~, what else might be hiding down there?

"As the years wore on, the Firstqueen, Life-Maker and Many-Mother, delighted in her people. Yet she grew sick with worry in her deepest heart. For in the shadows of the trees and the hidden seaside caves, death came unto her isle unbidden. For wherever her children met in places no one else could see, they would fall to blows. Only her voice, ringing clear and true from her tree-top keep, could stop them. When she called them to her court, neither could answer for their anger.

"Murder haunted her domain, brought not by the Outerliers 'cross the sea. Order's Fire was yet impure among her people. Chaos lingered even there, and so long as it did, no child would ever be safe. Not even those of her own blood, born of

Book II

Fires purest; for they all fought each other whenever her duties called her away. They grew older and stronger as the years trickled by, their brawls ever-more-dangerous, while she grew weaker and slower, a shadow of the once-called Dead-Maker. She knew her death would come, by the hands of time if not the hands of men, and when it did, her people would destroy themselves.

"When her fears had grown strongest and hopelessness hung heavy over the island of mankind, their end came from the sea. Behold: a giant with strength borne of Chaos' brightest tongue and years of battle, crossing the sea where hundreds more had failed. From the surf he rose, ten feet tall with beard and hair dyed red with the blood of a thousand foes. As he stared into the hateful torchlight, two fishermen saw him standing there. They cried alarm before the beast, unwearied, threw them down in death.

"Forth he came to battle, shattering the gates and charging for the Firstqueen's treetop fortress. One by one, the bravest rose to challenge him, holding bowls of seawater that he might see the truth and change – all to no avail. With naught but fist and oak-thick arm, the giant shed blood enough to drown the Vale. He stood but a moment over each kill, moving ever-towards the place where the Fire of Order burned brightest. There, he would extinguished it forever.

"The warriors of the Queen, few as they were, lay broken on the road as he reached the mighty castle roots. With a voice like bellows, he cried for the Firstqueen to come forth and die, come forth and face his wrath. If she refused, he swore that all her children would die before he tore her home up from its roots and hurled it into the sea."

Here, I finally did stop Kirlinder, just as Will jumped back into his seat with an eager grin on his face. *How could the giant call to the queen?* I asked. She'd invented her language, he said – she and the Firstking. How could an Outerlier know how to speak it? My tutor's lips opened... then drew tighter than usual. He turned to Will, then turned away just as quickly when he realized he was looking to an inferior for answers he didn't have. After a moment, he went on as though I hadn't asked the question. Will's face fell, but I smiled; seems priests really don't have all the answers.

"The Firstqueen heard the giant's words," he resumed, as Will drove the cart, rattling and jolting, down the makeshift ramp. "She saw the blood-soaked road from her keep, and her people, cowering in the shadows as they looked up towards her, their savior. She stared down at the raving monster as he kicked and flailed and shouted through his beard. In her youth, she'd been a warrior no less mighty than he; if she descended the ladder and faced him, she might emerge victorious. But she wasn't sure. She knew not what strength remained in her body, and she could not call upon her husband's aid: war, ship-making, and time's dark passage had rendered him infirm. If she fought and failed – or worse, if she succeeded – then her children would see her fighting her fellow man, and Chaos might blaze anew like embers buried beneath the ash. Yet if she remained aloft, this terrible foe would make good his promise. The flame of Order would pass from the Vale, and all life would drown in darkness.

"Sudden and terrible as her face in the starlight, she knew the answer. Turning from the window, she went to her husband, kissed his pale and trembling cheek, then mounted the ladder and climbed down towards death.

"The giant gave a lusty laugh to see the old woman climbing down, sensing how bright her holy light did burn, and was upon her in two strides, ready to snuff it out. She turned to face him. Long they studied one another, one with a searching, impatient glare, the other with a mother's gaze, looking for some spark of goodness. Then the Firstqueen of all the Vale bent, kneeling before him. Her people, emerging from the darkness, stared in disbelief as their Life-Maker handed herself over... and they along with her.

"In her heart, Order burned brighter than ever before, and her eyes blazed forth with holy light even before magyk came to be. Her voice, barely a whisper, rang in every ear as she spoke the first words of holy writ: 'Remember my mercies.'

"Her words carried across all the land – yet to the ears of her assassin, they meant nothing." Kirlinder squirmed as my eyes asked the same question as before. Again, I got no answer. "The champion of Chaos raised both his fists above his mighty head. The Life-Maker bowed lower, closed her eyes, and drew one final smile across her mother's face.

"The hands fell heavy. All breath fell still, all creatures, silent. Far above, the first star glimmered once more in the darkened firmament, then was gone forevermore.

"Silence died with screams of rage. Her true-born children were the first to charge, leaping at the murderer and pulling him down to the bloodied earth. Then came the rest, every one whom the Life-Maker had freed from Chaos' thrall, now crying for death, death, death. The giant, no longer facing the weak children he expected, reared and tried to throw them free. But they were too many, and his great strength was less than he imagined. Realizing his doom, he cried out in despair. Someone found a wide, sharp flint upon the road and raised it, ready to cut out the murderer's heart.

"It was then they heard the king. Against all hope, the dying lord had made it to the foot of the ladder on limbs too thin for such a climb. Sprawled across the dirt, clutching his beloved savior, lover, and friend, he wailed aloud... wailed for them to stop.

"They froze in disbelief. Even the giant ceased struggling. The King-Father's command tore at their every instinct. Surely, he would want this monster dead even more than they... had it not just murdered his wife?

61

"As tongues of Chaos and Order strove within their breasts, a suckling pig ran suddenly across the lane. One of the king's sons leapt upon the animal – much as you did farmer," Kirlinder said, adding his own words to his holy writ. "In his heart, he heard his mother's words as he seized the stony blade from his brother. Before disbelieving eyes, he slaughtered the pig, letting its blood run down the street in place of the giant's. Just loud enough to hear, he whispered, 'Remember her mercies.'"

Kirlinder paused there, nodding approval. "King's command and prince's sacrifice grew strong in the hearts of man, and the breeze which first sparked the Fire of Order in the Firstqueen rose to a tempest. The flame of Chaos shuddered and shrank, even in the heart of the giant. Rising from beneath the children of Order, who no longer desired his blood, he looked upon his work – and wept for all he'd done.

"He buried the Life-Maker in a sepulcher dug with his very hands. Every day, he learned of her mercies, and by the strength of his back and the work of many years, he transformed the island into a mighty city, carving great walls from the cliffside. And ever since that day, the swine is sacrificed in the Life-Maker's honor: for one must die that the many may live, and the flame of Order burn on.

"This," he whispered, eyes half shut, "is holy writ. This is the very good. Know it… and be at peace."

Does every story in this ~~blasted~~ book end like that? Telling you to believe it and forget your doubts? If they're all like these first two, then they certainly need to – otherwise, how could the church hold so much power? ~~Fire and Arches~~… savages discovering mercy by looking in a puddle? Inventing languages and building ships without any guide? Sparing a murderer because somebody else killed a pig – a pig which just happened to show up at exactly the right moment? I think of my own mother, distant though her memory may be; I had no one to blame for her death (besides my ~~damned~~ fool of a father who dragged her out to Halistoc), but if I had, nothing would've kept me from killing her murderer. Although...

There is one part of the story which rings true. The murderous gall rising in my throat at the thought of someone hurting mother (or Senaia, or Jayceson) is all-too-familiar; I tasted it once before on Crowntop, when I attacked Will. The memory is more horrible and ugly each time it returns. Kirlinder's talk of a killing instinct in the heart of man seems true enough; at least, true enough in mine. What took hold that night wasn't human... not human as I know it. I would've killed Will without knowing why, sure as the Firstqueen's children would've killed each other. Perhaps we do need sacrifice; perhaps it's good that I caught the pig, that Brook's knife cut it open... the "very good," even. I've seen men kill each other for sidelong glances and unspoken words. Even in Ellingston, people vanish beneath the lakes and rivers and unsown fields every year. Perhaps the sacrifice did kindle some good. Maybe someone was saved today by a sudden memory of the Firstqueen's mercies.

But that's the strangest part: she didn't even try to fight. She just went to her end as silent as the dreaming. The pig didn't choose to be sacrificed (or to be breakfast, for that matter), but she did. She sacrificed herself. To die – suffering in the place of another... could anyone really do that? Could I? Maybe. If Jayceson or Senaia... yes. I could die for them. I'm sure of that. It's all I'm certain of now, in the utter dark of the Rift. Even the stars have vanished overhead, and the campfire's burned to its last embers.

I could. I hope I would. I pray I never have to.

~the sacrificial rite in the rift was the first recorded outside the courts of the panopticon. it was also the first performed after the unexpected end of exhillion's reign~

The Gräzland Tales

Book II

V

I'm dead.

Oh, I'm still walking and breathing (and writing, of course), but only out of habit. My life has vanished into shadow and dream ever since I left Shellingor. Or Raligstae. Or even the Capital. Arches of the Earth, maybe I've always been dead, and never realized it 'til…

Dammit. Even at the end, I can't remember my teacher's advice… not even when I've no time to get lost in tale-telling. *End at the end* – how appropriate. It's unlikely anyone will ever read this little red book; not unless they're as lost as I am in this awful canyon. But still, I feel compelled to finish this tale. I owe him… well, much more than that, but this is all I can do.

Yestereve passed and morning came, with nightmares to chase off sleep. The camp was nearly the same as our last, if just a little smaller and surrounded by the concealing nooks which allowed my little rebellion. I woke to an odd silence. Kirlinder had cast the all-too-familiar sapping spell after supper (I'd begun to worry about its long-lasting effects), but it faded as usual when I sat upright. The morn was peaceful, especially compared to the yester… or was it ante-yester? It's impossible to say: all light is gone now, save the one I write by. Even that is dying fast.

I climbed out of my tent. The priests were practicing their

usual silence, sitting criss-cross on the ground around the fire, hoods up, backs to me. It looked as though I'd wandered into a forest of large, black mushrooms sprouting low and fat from the stone. I almost laughed before I thought better of it, and glanced around for any sign of my tutor. There was none. I let the chuckle loose.

A full third of the priests whirled 'round, abandoning their meditations to glare at me with less-than-edifying thoughts. Even so, they said not a word as I wound between them to the pot of Panopticon porridge hanging over the sallow magefire; no bonfires that day (or sacrifices, thank goodness). I felt the daggers in my back disappear as they quietly resumed their ruminations and I spooned my prisoner's portion (or a bit more) into an unused bowl.

Their silence was catching once I got my morning mischief out. Unable to cross my legs quite the way they did, I first stood, ignoring the creeping awkward feeling of towering over my captors, then knelt, resting on both knees before the fire. The posture was uncomfortable, but not because of the cold, hard floor (at least, not entirely). It was the nearest to praying I'd been in many a year. Eating my dutiful breakfast, balancing the bowl upon my lap, I began to wonder if…

Arches, the wind just snapped up; nearly blew the fire out. No time for wonderings – tell what happened, start to end.

Will and Kirlinder were nowhere to be seen, but Will was young and Kirlinder was an old man. Butchery is tiring work, or so I've heard. I didn't expect them to rise until late morning, so even in the oppressive silence, I didn't hear them coming until their boots appeared before me. I glanced up from where I knelt; they, at least, didn't feel uncomfortable standing over their fellows. Nor did they respect their silence… at least, not Kirlinder.

"G'morn, farmer!" came the uncharacteristically cheerful greeting from my teacher. Will whispered the same, standing two paces back from his master and five paces clear of me. He still had a bandage 'round his head; freshly soiled, as though his wound had broken open in the night. In the firelight, the whole thing looked red.

The strange new undergrowth of our camp leapt to life at the sound of Kirlinder's voice (some rather clumsily, tripping on their cloaks). Suddenly, I was the only one not standing. Rocking back on my heels, I jumped up quick as I could. The already-dark world darkened as I did, and the sound of ringing bells returned to my ears. Our captain turned, giving a sharp command to strike the camp which I only half-heard. The priests stirred the otherwise stagnant air as they rushed to fulfil his order. No one wanted to linger.

Despite his cheery smile, Kirlinder let the weary silence fall over the camp again. He made no talk, small or otherwise, while I spooned the last of my waterlogged oats down my throat. They were even less appetizing under his scrutiny. He took none for himself; perhaps he thought yesterday's indulgence required fasting to follow. Will took a helping, though – his and Kirlinder's, by the look of it. He wolfed the flavorless mush down once he'd found a seat some distance from us both. Kirlinder's dissecting stare didn't break as I finished my meal, set my bowl aside, and went to the wagon. His eyes stayed fixed on me as he climbed aboard; they only broke away when Will took the driver's seat, shattering the silence with a bloated belch. Kirlinder whirled at the rude sound. I couldn't help another laugh. Will apologized, and whipped Phil into motion.

I didn't even try to meet my teacher's eyes; I just busied mine with the ever-shifting lines in the walls and the way the torchlight played strange games across them. My gaze lingered on one or two wide ledges. As we wound deeper into the canyon, I kept hearing footsteps up above, too light and quick for humans, and whispers which could've been the wind. I didn't tell Kirlinder; I was still holding ideas of hope and rescue, damned fool that I was.

After what felt like a quarter-hour, Kirlinder inhaled (perhaps the first time he'd breathed all day) and cleared his throat. I turned from the shadows. His eyes were keen as ever, but they shone with curiosity. "You've many questions, farmer," he said. "Many indeed." I watched in disbelief (and gratitude) as he pulled the red-backed primer from his satchel and handed it to me. "Ask them."

I snatched the booklet (whose pages I no longer need to worry about exhausting) from his hand. He expected me to open it and ask the questions written there; I suspected he spent the night before finding ready answers for them. I didn't need to lift the covers… though I did, just for the comfort of seeing my own writing (how he could read it is a mystery I'll never solve). The questions I'd put down (and a hundred more besides) pressed against my mind, spilling out all at once at the unlooked-for invitation. *What were the Fires made of? Where did they come from? Who lit them? Does Chaos still burn in the Outerliers? In us? What kind of boats did the Firstking make? How many? Who was the prince who killed the pig, and why…*

And so on and so on. Kirlinder's smile (so oft misjudged as smug) dipped. Some of my questions were so obvious, he already knew the answers. He couldn't answer the rest; not unless you count mumbling something about "faith" an answer. When I finally ran short of questions (or breath), Kirlinder leapt at the opportunity, setting a comforting hand on my shoulder. Until that moment, I would've recoiled – but he spoke slowly and softly, so quiet that Will couldn't hear him across the bench. "My child," he began, again sounding like the father in Raligstae, "these scriptures are strange, I will not deny. I've questioned the holy writ myself, with such doubts as you now feel." Somehow I doubted that – but I let

Book II

it pass. "And yet – time and again – those doubts reach the same conclusion. Even if the writ be false, man needs it still, like food and air and sacrifice. That's what really matters, farmer: faith."

My eyebrows rose at the word. He'd read my journal, knew my opinion of it all-too-well. He chuckled. "Yes farmer: faith," he said, nodding. "Belief. Hope. A longing for more than this vain, short life. If man can believe things will be better, then perhaps he'll make them better – even if what he hopes for never comes. Without faith..." He waved his hand at the shadows around us. Will craned his neck, trying to listen in. "Without faith, man is lost in the moonless night of the Dark Days. Always, I remember that," he said, putting both hands on my shoulders like a comforting parent, "and believe anew."

Will cried out in pain. A pale shaft stood buried between his shoulder and his neck, flown from one of the alcoves above. Will clawed at the arrow, already staining red, as another sailed by, striking the place in the bed of the wagon where I'd been hidden. The reins slipped from his fingers as a third whistled by so close that the fletchings cut his ear. Kirlinder and I watched helplessly as he flinched, lost balance, and fell from the wagon.

"ÆLFAL!" Kirlinder screamed. My mouth hung open as white arrows with black eagle feathers fell in earnest, raising screams of stomach-turning pain. "TREACHERY!" he cried above the panic, "Defend Yourselves!"

In the brief moment light endured, I saw the two priests marching in front of us: one caught an arrow in the chest, but the other snapped up like a schoolboy at his master's command, throwing his torch into the riverbed. Just before it went dark, I saw him reach for the pendant at his neck. Kirlinder tossed ours aside; it hissed and sputtered as he grabbed the reins to keep them from being dragged under the cart. The nightmares flickering on the walls vanished. The priest ahead of us ejected the thin red wafer from his necklace, pinched it between his fingers, and set it on his tongue. In his dark cloak, he vanished almost entirely; then two points of deadly blue shone forth as we sailed past him. Phil hardly needed Kirlinder's whipping.

The torchlight wasn't missed for long: a brilliant, wavering white took its place, filling the canyon. I turned back to see ranks of holy men spread out along the ravine, arms raised, eyes shining, lips moving. The other wagon's driver struggled to keep their mule from following Phil's example and trampling the priests. Some stood, but most lay sprawled across the stones with white arrows in their arms and legs, screaming... or else silent and unmoving. I saw Will crawling for the canyon wall; it was the last I saw of him.

A sound like rain on a tin roof rose above the howls of pain. I looked up; a blanket of cold light, looking almost like liquid, bisected the dark walls above, growing dimmer or brighter where the arrows stuck and shattered on the shielding spell. The clatter of steel on Arch-glass disappeared... but Kirlinder didn't slow. If anything, he snapped the reins harder against the poor animal's back. He knew what was coming long before I realized it was happening.

The high, terrible whinny of a beast far mightier than Phil's kin echoed after us as we reached the bend in the canyon. Half of the priests (half the ones still standing) turned away from their incantation at the noise. The rest struggled to hold the shield without them as, out of the dark behind them, an impossibly tall, thin rider appeared on an impossibly thin, tall horse. Rider, horse, sword, and armor were pale as the arrows of the unseen archers, nearly glowing in the magyked light.

Ælfs was all my mind could register, before it realized: *They've found us.* Then, chasing that: *They've found* him.

Book II

The priests vanished from my sight behind the canyon wall. The thundering hooves of a hundred riders rose behind us. The crackle of shattering arrows slowed, then vanished with the light. The wagon hurtled madly 'round the next corner. Clashing steel and crackling explosions echoed 'tween the dark walls, mingled with panicked braying as Phil drew us further and further away. He charged blind, hardly noticing the tug of the reins as Kirlinder tried to guide, then slow, his course. It was no use: he was deaf to all but instinct, as I was on Crowntop.

The half-cart swung from wall to wall, wheels throwing cold water over us as they fell into the river's narrow channel. I grit my teeth, trying not to bite through my tongue. *Hile! Hile!* Kirlinder kept shouting, pulling back the reins. There was no way to gauge our speed, save by the sickening lurches as it increased. Time was lost in the darkness. We'd turned into a passageway branching off into the Rift-stone, I realized. The line of sky above had vanished.

Not sure how I noticed that in the midst of my terror. I turned back for a moment, trying to see where we'd turned wrong – not my best choice. But even if I'd been looking forward, I wouldn't have been able to see the outcropping leap up and smash our right wheel to splinters. I did heard the crunch, though. It sounded like breaking bone.

My stomach lurched anew as the wagon dropped sideways, dragging on its one remaining wheel before it struck another fissure. The cart flipped over, flinging us to the merciless stone. The reins snapped. Free of our weight, Phil (blind to our peril as everything else) bolted, imagining freedom at the end of the black tunnel. I wish him well, but that poor beast will never taste Capital hay again.

For once I was fortunate, if only compared to others: I was thrown clear of the wagon, skidding to a stop several feet away. Feeling every one of my brittle bones (unbroken, thank the Fires), I pushed myself upright. I'd come to a stop against one of the canyon walls – or bounced off it, more like. Something trickled down my face. For a moment, I thought it might be a tear, and went to wipe it away. Whatever it was, it ran warm and sticky from my brow. I looked at my hand. I could barely see my fingers, much less the color of what stained them. By the light of this last fire so many hours later, they're crusted red.

My eyes soon adjusted to the dark, like a dwarfish in his mine. I could just make out the wagon, overturned on the far side of the canyon… the wagon, the reins, and Kirlinder. He lay pinned between the stone and the side of the cart. Even if I hadn't seen him, I could've guessed at his trouble; as shock faded and he found his voice, it rose in screams of agony.

His cry woke the last of my dazed senses. I leapt to my feet and ran (or rather limped) to his side. The cart had fallen across the lower part of his back, crushing him beneath its weight. Squatting down, I slipped my fingers underneath and leveraged all my strength (little as that was) and all my weight. It was just barely enough: the cart rose, and Kirlinder pulled himself free with his arms. His legs were no help – they dragged uselessly behind him as he crawled out. My guts turned at the sight: something told me they wouldn't move again.

The cart slipped out of my fingers just as his boots were clear. I tottered back, spun, and fell against its wooden side, gasping for air. The atmosphere was even heavier in the tunnel. Kirlinder took no such rest; despite the pain, he dragged himself across the canyon floor. In the strangled light, I saw why: his satchel, which had never left his side, was lying against the opposite wall. He was already grabbing it before I gathered enough breath to call out: a wheezing, strangled *Stop!*

He didn't listen. His fingers clawed at the bag, caught it, and

Book II

tore it open. His desperation was clear, more painful to him than his useless legs or shattered back... though perhaps he didn't feel anything there at all. The bag's contents were spread out on the stone in a moment: maps and purses and books of all shapes and sizes (one looking strangely like my old journal, come to think of it). His satchel deflated, and so did he. Flipping it over, he shook it out, nearly sticking his head inside for a better look at its dark and empty corners. He turned, legs not turning with him, as I finally found my feet (with a little help from the wagon). His lips flapped noiselessly as I made my ever-so-painful way over to him, stooped down, and slung his arm 'round my shoulder. A week ago, he carried me out of the Kingshead much the same way; he offered no more resistance than I had.

I dragged him back to the cart, leaning him gingerly against it. In the quiet of the canyon, I heard a squeaking, creaking sound: the remaining wheel, spinning uselessly in the air. "The prince!" He shouted suddenly. I'd lain back against the wagon, sliding down beside him; he latched onto my jacket with more force than I thought he could manage. "The prince is gone!" he croaked, eyes only inches from mine. "He must've... he could've... they... they must've taken him! Fire and Arches, they've..."

He cut off, either from shock or the sheepish look creeping over my face. Fear vanished from his eyes as confusion took its place. It was then that I finally confessed: my last genuine confession, or perhaps my first. They didn't take the prince – *I* did.

His white-knuckle grip slacked just enough to let me reach into my coat. I pulled the secondvessel from its familiar place above my heart. I couldn't help a sigh of relief when I saw it hadn't shattered in the fall. Another smile from Lady Fortune, I suppose.

Getting him from Kirlinder hadn't been easy; he wasn't so

gullible as I imagined, and the prince never left his side. I tried slipping my hand into his bag whenever I "accidentally" bumped shoulders with him, but his hand went straight to his satchel every time. I don't know why I was trying to steal him back. Perhaps I thought I could finish my mission alone once escape or rescue came. Perhaps I just wanted to annoy my teacher. Whatever the case, when the chance came, I took it. As we entered the Rift and our eyes adjusted to the shadows between sunlight and torchlight, the wagon rolled over a fallen boulder and jolted left. Kirlinder fell against Will, and I against Kirlinder. My quick fingers haven't forgotten their skill in all the years since Felliswell.

His eyes were wide as Will's had been on Crowntop. They turned from the prince, to me, to the bag, then back to my guilty grin before…

"Go! Run!" he sputtered. Flecks of spit (or something else) landed on my face. "Take him and GO!" Like Phil, I hardly needed to be told. I nodded, and he let go of my coat. I turned to wind his arm back 'round my neck…

"NO!" His cry knocked me back. He coughed (much of his strength spent), then; "No. I'll only slow you. They're…" His old voice cracked. He grabbed the pentaform at his neck, popped the latch, and threw the tablet back without ceremony. A dull fire kindled amidst the shadows 'cross his face. "You have to get out. There's more… more priests. Waiting, up north. Find them… find…"

I stared in disbelief. Did the old man expect me to let him die in the dark? Did he really think I could? The far-off sound of hooves grew louder every second. Even so, I couldn't tear my eyes from Kirlinder.

His pained expression twisted with inhuman fury. His eyes blazed from the shadows. "*GO!*"

I went. That one word held all the power of a general and all the wisdom of a teacher, and I couldn't disobey. Forgetting both his pain and mine, I turned and ran. And ran. And ran. My heart hammered loud enough to drown out all sound – almost all sound. At my back, a thunder of horses and magyk shook the tunnel. Stumbling, bouncing from wall to wall, I ran blind, save for the flashes of white which drove my shadow far ahead of me. I could not, would not, stop; not even to think what I was running towards.

Light burst behind me, taking what was left of my sight. The shattering report shook the stones, and a blast of unnatural wind tore down the passage. It didn't send me flying, but I toppled, flat on my palms, as it struck me square in the back. The tunnel shook like earth in an Arch-quake. I clenched everything I could, fearing the roof above me would collapse. The stone slowly stopped its trembling, until everything lay still as death.

I lay blind, deaf, and bleeding from hands, head, and Fires-know where else. One by one, my senses found their way home. High voices with an odd accent cursed far away in the dark – or else screamed in that same register. All sounds of battle had vanished: Kirlinder had brought the walls down on top of them... and himself.

I reached that conclusion after about an hour of blind running, as I finally collapsed in a heap of sweat and tears and was not immediately overtaken by Ælfali horses. After all I did and said of him, he gave his life to save mine. To save the mission. What a bloody waste.

I ran as far as my legs could carry me. The roof fell lower and lower and the walls nearer and nearer. If I went any further, I'd have to crawl. I'd hoped for some glimmer of sunlight, some kiss of the fresh-air outside. I found neither: the cave only led deeper into the Rift-stone, and Kirlinder put a wall between me and any chance of escaping with the prince. My knees buckled as I realized the truth, and I collapsed in a poor imitation of prayer for the second time that day.

I don't know how long I wallowed in grief for myself, my teacher, and his pointless sacrifice... Arches, I even mourned the prince. I'm sorry Alexi: I cannot free you. Not as you wished. Not the way you deserve.

I haven't the time to describe what I thought and felt in that senseless void where all light had been forgotten. Eventually I did rise. With nowhere else to go, I walked back up the cavern, one hand on the wall. After a moment, it brushed against an old, dry tree, sprouted through the stone in the endless dark. My journal was still tucked into my pocket, along with a few stray matches from the king's pack. I took my best guess at which pages were still blank, and tore out three. It's by the light of the fire they kindled that I finish this last record of the mission to the Gräzlands. I'm unsure how my own story will end (though hunger or thirst seem the most likely causes), but there's no one left to write it in any case. I propped Alexi on a nearby shelf of stone, where he could watch me write. The Rift's a grand sepulcher for both of us; even if neither of us would've chosen it. So it goes.

I have a little light left to scratch some final words – not that they'll be remembered, unless some hapless fool comes tumbling over the rocks and finds this little red volume, still clutched in my rotted hand. Even so, I need to write something. Perhaps they'll be heard in the Dreamlands... or perhaps not. But even so...

Jayceson, my dear son: if ever you read this, you've already grown into the man you'll be without me. Do not doubt that man. Whatever the years may make of you, I know it shall bring to the full all I see in your youth. Begrudge me not the years I missed. Know that I meant what I last said to you in the market square: I love you. Though I said I'd see you soon, know, my son, that I never meant to lie.

Senaia, my beloved: so you were and are and ever shall be.

Book II

So long as this heart beats, it beats for you alone. Forgive me every waking moment that I spent away from you. I know you'll wait unto the fading of the sun for me... but don't. There is nothing I desire more but that your days be full and your nights be rich, even if I cannot share them. Take them all for yourself, for you are everything. Keep my memories strong, but never live within them.

Kirlinder, my teacher, my friend: how could I be so wrong? I called you captor, kidnapper, and thief, but you cared for me more than Brook. I cheated and mocked, fought and stole... and still you gave your life for me. I'm sorry I wasted it, and sorrier still that I was so unworthy of your friendship.

Brook: I know not if you live. If you do, pray find some peace. Whatever you've done, whatever you may be, you deserve that much. If you're not... then I hope to see you in what dreams await, and hope they're glad: we've both had too much of nightmares.

Your majesty, oh noble King Grett: you get the last of the light. You always seem to take the last: the last of the crop, the last of the coin, and the last of this farmer's life. You sent me (and Fires-know how many priests) to a cold and lonely death. The Lost-Ones were right to fear you. Your heart may burn with Fires true, but your compass stones cannot seem to steer it right. I owe you fealty, fidelity, loyalty... but not love. Know you have none from the man who gave everything in your service, and think better of your people. That much you owe...

> *~a handful of priests fled the battle and slipped past the ælfen rearguard. kirlinder was not among them~*

Book II

VI

Now, with far less excitement than I should feel, I confess that announcing my own death was somewhat premature. It's been some time since I wrote my last entry, and its dire tone might seem laughable... if only I didn't face much the same fate. When the firelight ran out before the blank pages of the notebook, I felt a thrill of vain hope: maybe, just maybe, there was more story to be told. I'd never been so superstitious before, and I don't intend to be again. Though I was right, the story's far from hopeful.

Sleep came easy in the utter dark, a sleep I didn't imagine I'd wake from. So too came the nightmares; black robes, chains, death, death... death. I'm finally certain what those cryptic lines written in the dead of that long-past night mean. I've still not seen the face of my pursuer, but when I woke, I couldn't shiver off the feeling that I didn't want to.

I opened my eyes. A strange inverse of my dream appeared: a white silhouette in place of a black one, against a backdrop of eternal night. There wasn't enough light to see it clearly, but its skin, hair, and clothes shone in the dark like sun through torn curtains, and it held a pale sword. Sleep didn't stop my throat that morning: I screamed at a rather undignified pitch as terror poured cold down my spine.

The ælfen scout made a noise like a stepped-on mouse and rushed towards me with no more sound than a mouse might make. A long, spindly hand covered my mouth. The grip wasn't terribly strong, but the pressure beneath his fingertips was so great that I feared he might leave bruises, crushing my cheeks against my jaw. "Quít shoutíng, fül," said a squeaking voice from somewhere in the hazy patch of white hovering in front of me, ""Sease, or be kíll-ed." He lifted his long, cruel sword, barely visible in the dark, for emphasis. He hardly needed to: I understood his threat clearly enough, even with his heavy accent. I *quít* struggling just as fast as I could.

His vice-grip didn't slacken. The half-seen face turned back up the tunnel, and a piercing whistle sounded from unseen lips. I only heard it for one painful moment before it rose higher than mortal man could hear. *Ælfcall*, I thought, struggling to breath beneath his grip. Despair overtook wonder: there were more ælfs coming. *Arches*. I heard fast-approaching footfalls in the tunnel, soft and quick as the ones I heard before the attack.

At least they brought light with them. For a moment, I thought it was sunlight, somehow reappearing 'round the corner. It looked too cold and steady to be torchlight, and yet it was: a long, curved handle of carved and polished stone glimmered where it held a tongue of white-hot mage-fire which neither wavered nor fluttered nor gave off any smoke. I thought Brook's little iron torches were a miracle, but this… this was ælf-magyk: rarely seen by men who lived to tell the tale.

So entrancing was the flame that I didn't notice who held it. The ælfen troupe was standing over me by the time I took my eyes off the dazzling device. Their uniforms were all tight-fit and sheer-white leather, darkened only at the seams and beneath their bright steel buttons. They were made in sections, with the longest flap angled across their chests from shoulder to hip. A dizzying array of straps, belts, and cords held the pieces together yet allowed them to slide freely, despite the second-skin fit. I've had many chances to examine the costume up close: every ælf, regardless of rank, wears the same uniform. It makes Warden armor look like peasant roughspun.

"Yü dæmn-ed fül," their captain, whose rank was marked only by a circlet 'round his shock-black hair, hissed at the scout, "a'whah hold yü hím so?" He pointed at me (more specifically, at the hand across my mouth). The scout follow his gesture, saw the shade of blue I was turning, and released his grip. I gasped, offering an unheard *thanks* to my so-called rescuer (I'd call him something else, but I already used up every variation of "kidnapper" on Kirlinder, unfair as it was).

"He was shoutíng awe-full lou'd," he explained, jumping up and making an attempt to straighten his uniform or dust it off, immaculate as it looked. "We do-en't know if there are anah'more of these," he glared down at me (quite a long ways down), "*Prahsts*." He said it like a curse.

I swallowed as best as I could with my mouth dry from running, weeping, and screaming, and just barely got out that I wasn't... a priest, that is. That earned me a disgusted look from the scout and a laugh from the captain, as though he'd never heard anything so funny. His voice sounded like that of a girl just out of dolls, and his laugh was painful. I'm sure he doesn't use it often – not if he's kept his command for a very long time. It'd be enough to make me mutiny, if I had to endure that sound every day.

"No?" he said, finally addressing me, "Not a'prahst, say yü?" His sword, made from the same strange mineral as the torch and one piece from point to pommel, rose gracefully to the knot in my throat. It felt deadly sharp and strangely warm. "Then a'whah tress-pæsses yü æmid'st these – these... *retrogrætes?*" I didn't catch the curse the first time (an old ælfen word, if ever I heard one – which I hadn't), but he made his meaning clear, pulling a bundle of brass chains from his belt. In the steady torchlight, the pentaforms shone rose as

81

they hung open and empty.

Another laugh (and another terribly stupid urge to punch him in the face) tortured my ears before he tucked his trophies away. "Or do yü expec-et me to belle-eve yü ære'n-ot a'man, but a'fore-short'n-ed ælf? And a'glutt'n-üss one at that?" His soldiers joined in on his third outburst, either accustomed to their captain's shrill laughter or too afraid to speak their minds. They sounded like blackjays on a hot summer's day.

The soldiers stopped laughing long before their captain, but even he seemed cut short when he noticed my reaction – or the lack thereof. Though I didn't appreciate what he implied about my waistline, I didn't have anything to look guilty about. Clearly, I wasn't a priest. Surely he could see that?

"Heh," he said, the last note of his laugh coming out as a question. "So – not a'prahst, then. So a'who and a'what, and a'whah are yü…" His eyes, dark as his striking hair, turned from my face to my clothes, my boots, and my calluses. They widened as he finally saw past my race and weight. "The far-mér?"

It was mangled in the accent of the holy city, but that didn't stop me from nodding emphatically as I could with a blade against my throat. Its point felt sharp enough to cut the air itself.

The captain turned, looking to each of his troops as he tried to mask his confusion. They all looked puzzled as he. He turned back quickly. "The far-mér? Yü cae'n-ot be. The fahre of Shell-ín-gor…"

I opened my mouth to explain that Kirlinder had saved me from the blaze; then I stopped. They knew. They knew who I was, they knew where I'd been, they knew where the priests were going and how to catch them unawares… someone had betrayed us. Betrayed the king. Someone in his own court. And if they knew what I was carrying…

Uncertainty vanished from the captain's eyes. "Search hím." His company leapt at the order. What followed was one of the most uncomfortable experiences I can remember. They seized my arms, heaving me to my feet before posing me like some city-brat's plaything. I winced: long, cold fingers reached in and found places even Senaia's never touched. They lifted and padded and prodded, probing every crease and fold, and I prayed some aftershock from Kirlinder's spell might collapse the walls around us and put a merciful end to it all. It could only have lasted a few minutes, but it felt like an eternity on the rack.

I endured, refusing to forget my mission. As they turned me around to search my back side, I saw the rocky shelf across from the pale, dry tree. I'd set the secondvessel there last night so I could see it while I wrote. In the light of the ælf-torch, an empty ledge stared back.

I groaned aloud... louder than I should've. I worried the captain might hear my despair and decide to search out the prince, wherever he'd fallen. My... situation, however, did an admirable job disguising the reason for the noise. The soldiers finally turned me back around, reporting that I didn't have it. Suspicion brewed in the captain's eyes. "Then a'why should they spare yü?" His high, smooth brow crinkled painfully as he thought. "Could'n-ot be mercah – the *retrogrætes* hæd none." His fist tightened as he cursed their memory. I might've risen to their defense, had his sword not risen first to the place above my ribs. "There mu-st be a reason." The creases on his scalp turned downwards as he spoke. "Else yü wouldn-ot be here. Confess ít, far-mér."

That title was growing more and more grating, but even so, I confessed: confessed that I knew nothing. I had no earthly notion why Kirlinder had dragged my sorry weight along, besides the *mercah* he so clearly rejected. I could see no other explanation for Kirlinder's final kindness.

I said as much to the captain, in softer terms than I'm known for. Clearly, he wanted a different answer. He sighed, teasing the sword up slightly as though toying with the idea of running me through – then spoke."Fine." His voice shrank to a sinister whisper. "If that is how yü wish ít, there are a'manah in Ælfal who-ed make yü weep to tell." He cocked his head to his soldiers, still holding my arms as though I could've even tried to run. "Bríng hím."

The company led me out of the canyon... Arches, I wish I could write that. They certainly could've: I had no desire to linger in its dark reaches. Instead, they dragged me out by my weary arms. They had to, once they cinched a heavy canvas sack over my head. Turns out the blind demanded a less gentle guidance than others. Perhaps I could've felt my way after them, following what torchlight slipped through the blindfold – had they not wrapped my wrists in cords so tight and wire-thin they drew blood. Yet again, I was carried like some rebellious prisoner in a direction I was more than willing to go.

I made the passage blind once more, with two ælf soldiers crushing my arms and my feet striking unseen fissures as we marched on all-too-fast. I didn't see the place where Kirlinder took his last stand, so I couldn't tell how it had been cleared... only that it had. New, ælfen voices and the sounds of their horses signalled that we'd reached the Rift, and I realized we hadn't climbed over any fallen stones. I've heard rumors of ælfen half-breeds: monsters brought back from the Dark Days which wield earth-tearing strength. Maybe they cleared our path.

Of course, I didn't see any such creatures. I didn't see anything. Besides a few more points of torchlight which joined ours, my world was black (and terribly itchy). Some of the voices called out greetings, and the captain called back; both in Ælfen. One said something which sounded an awful lot like *g'morn* (*g-mürn'n* is what I heard), and I realized a full day had passed since the attack.

We stopped. The pleasant greetings stopped too, replaced by a stern, steady, yet still high-pitched voice. Whoever it belonged to (I never saw his face, or any of the ælfen faces, long enough to put names to them) clearly took note of my species and disapproved of it. "a'whah bríng yü a man ínto our companah, captain?" He'd switched to low Valeian, his voice sharp as it could be while still stretching out its words. "Did'n-ot yü heár mah or'd-ers?"

I heard the captain shuffling; bowing apologetically, I guessed (the torchlight dipped a little lower). "Apologies, mah'lord. Yür or'd-ers were for a'*prahsts* we fou'nd. 'tis'n-ot a prahst, sír."

There was a moment's silence from the whole Rift, as if the stones themselves listened in. I could feel the commander's anatomizing gaze even through the blinding bag pulled a little too tight 'round my neck. "Yü do'n-ot thínk," he finally spoke, "that I woüld belle-eve thís creatüre ís..."

For a moment, I prayed he wouldn't *belle-eve* the captain's word; I've done an inordinate amount of that in the last few days. Surely, I couldn't be the Gräzlander he'd heard so much about (from whom, I'd like to know)... he'd burned to death in Shellingor. By the Dome, I didn't even have the secondvessel!

"a'what would yü do wíth ít?" My hope shattered on his words; seems I've left a trail of broken hopes behind. The captain switched to Ælfen, probably to keep me from running off in panic. I already knew what he was planning: Ælfal, dungeons, torture, and, inevitably, death.

The commander gave some approval (a sound between a grunt and a sigh) and we were moving again, towards the tramping hooves and restless snorting further up the Rift. The ælfs must've built a makeshift livery in the canyon: it sounded (and smelled) like two dozen horses were crowded in around us. The cacophony drowned out all other noise. The grip on my arms tightened and my boots left the cold stone as I was laid stomach-first across something round and warm. It shifted with the unexpected weight. My wrists parted slightly as the cords were loosed, then immediately tied off to something behind me. Unable to move, much less resist, I felt another set winding 'round my ankles. Before I could protest, I was bound to one of the horses' saddles. The soldiers who'd put me there let go, and the cords bit flesh as I fell. I wouldn't slip the binds mid-gallop, no matter what I tried.

There was a moment's pause (I wondered if they planned to just leave me there to soften me up), then the horse canted sideways, whinnying as one of the soldiers swung up into the saddle and added his weight (little as it was) to mine. Another ælfcall rose in the canyon, vanishing behind the sound of hooves. The animal shuddered at the painful noise before the captain cried out. "Thund-ér ín Firah!" he screamed in his high, ælfen voice. *Firah ín Thund-ér!* the rider (and several dozen others) replied. The captain gave one more irritating crack of laughter before the crash of hooves and a lurching rush of speed drowned out all my senses.

This week began in the back of a cart, unable to move. It ended on the back of a horse, trussed up like a saddlebag and battered to breathlessness. *Belle-eve yü me,* the backsides of Ælfali steeds are no more comfortable than any others'. Faster than I thought possible, the horse reached a full, reckless gallop, and I bounced up and down with every fall of its crashing hooves. The remnants of my last meal (such as it was) sloshed the other way. Had our pace slowed during the day, I'm certain it would've sprayed across the other riders a half-step behind us. *Firah ín Thund-ér,* indeed; the closeness of the canyon made them loud enough to shatter stone. At every drop and turn, I was sure the ropes would fail and I'd make a neat little mess beneath the Ælfali purebreds. No such luck.

The sickened feeling in my stomach (already rising to my throat) mingled with the worry growing there. Ælfal… the wonder from beyond the Vale, the home of the ælfkind. Ælfal… the most beautiful place no mortal man can seen and live to tell. I knew what waited for me there, and dreaded it no less with every passing hour… yet even so, I couldn't keep my roiling mind from squealed with delight. Soon (very soon), I'd see what lay behind the forbidden walls of the highfolk's capital.

I knew we left the Rift when the blackness of the blindfold turned a lighter grey and our course turned right – west, and straight for our fearful end. Our pace somehow quickened: I guess they didn't want to be seen on the open plain so near the Gräzland border with a human captive in tow… especially if Grett's made good on his plans and mustered his army to the south. Somewhere amidst the rib-cracking course of their headlong charge, I wondered how long the horses could keep their master's pace.

As long as they demanded it, apparently. The horse was too breathless to whinney in pain; the rider called *Ní! Ní! Ní!* as he kicked and snapped the reins. When it felt like we could go no further, we finally – mercifully – began to slow. My brain felt like it was rolling loose inside my skull as we crested the short rise at the end of the day's journey; the curses, oaths, and supplications pouring through it reached a crescendo as we came to an all-too-sudden stop and dismounted.

Correction: the rider dismounted, leaping from the saddle. His hands (or the hands of some other ælf, I had no way of knowing) scrambled at the ropes, loosing each knot in rapid sequence. It wasn't fast enough: the run-out, rung-out horse dropped with a sickening thud (tossing me up and down once more for good measure) and rolled over on its flank. My teeth clapped together, but my captor managed to pull me away before I was crushed. He cursed (*Arch-és*), slapping the poor animal before going back to fiddling with the cords. The last knot popped as the tension released, and I toppled, face-first, into a mound of fresh snow. For the first time in what seemed like a year, I felt the icy bite of the cold, damp blanket of winter.

I didn't vomit as I'd feared, either grown accustomed to the torturous bouncing or too empty-stomached to be emptied. Perhaps the former was more likely; I lay shaking and jittering as though I were still on the horse for a good long while. The soldier laughed sharp and quick at the sight, then stood, crunching through the snow as he walked off. *No no, don't bother – I'll get up myself*, my rankled mind called after him. I was shuddering and blind but for the hazy impression of the westering sun poking through the bag.

The image exploded without warning as the bag was ripped off by another soldier. I hadn't even heard him approach. The cables 'round my ankles disappeared just as quick while I blinked, reeling at the invasion of day, fading into evening as it was. The ropes around my wrists remained; the soldier used them to haul me to my feet and lead me to a grove of northern deadwoods at the edge of the narrow ridge. It was only the following morn that I realized we were camped on the Rift-stone itself, on an outcropping in its easternmost face… well within Ælfali territory, and well beyond any human help.

Of course I didn't realize where we were at first: soon as we reached the skeletal trees (one was already being dragged away for firewood), my hands were loosed, pulled behind the trunk, and lashed back together. I was too dazed to realize what they were doing until new ropes were likewise secured around my legs, chest, and ankles. The soldier marched off in clear self-satisfaction, and I was left standing there, blinded by the merciless sun with my back against a hard, chafing pillar.

I was only blinded for a few moments; as the day bedded down beyond the far-off Steps, I was finally able to turn my eyes back up. Rising above the endless, rolling snowfield (a welcome enough sight in itself), alone on the blasted plain and glittering like frozen fire in the sunset, stood Ælfal. A rush took me at the sight; fear and wonder mixed, as they so often do. I had only the briefest glimpse of it that evening, and an even briefer one come morning. Its spires and towers were blue and dim, hidden by the cold air between us. Even so, they were every bit as beautiful as I'd imagined. Obris had painted a glorious picture of the city in words, yet it fell utterly short of what I saw, looking down on it some decades later.

And yet fear remained. I'm a coward: I admit it freely, on and off the page. It's my lot to be terrified of a world which neither asks nor wants my part in it. Why should I rise against my fears – rise to them? Half of them (freezes and plagues and wild things) are kept at bay by the priests; the other half comes from the lordlings. To try and fight those is treason, and a short trip to the gibbet. Fear is the duty of me and my ilk.

I passed the quiet watches of the night alone, alternating between trying to make the trunk comfortable and staring across the plain to what I could still see of the city beneath the mother's moon. I couldn't keep myself from imagining all the horrible instruments of torture which waited there, invented by ælf-minds and built by ælf-magyk: devices too terrible to name and too cruel to use on their own kind. What sleep I got (a half-hour at most) was shallow and dreamless. At least I can be thankful the night-terrors didn't bleed into the dawn again, though this old corpse is growing weary of uneven patterns of sleep and sleeplessness.

I was awake before the sun, but a little after my captors. As the familiar Skar-stained yellow lit the towers of Ælfal, I heard a hurried flurrying behind me. I didn't wait long to be untied – as with everything they do (with the exception of speaking), speed was paramount. Boots crunched in the snow just before the rope around my chest tightened, loosened, and fell away... along with all the others holding me up. I stumbled forward, one stiff leg in front of the other, before the long, cold night of standing took its toll and I fell to the snow, unable to catch myself. The ælf laughed cruelly; my nose felt just as bruised as my pride.

Yet again, the ælf-laugh cut off sharply (time's too valuable to waste on laughter, it seems) before the cords around my wrists were re-tightened. Again, the ropes made an easy handle, and again, I was lifted and pushed towards what remained of the camp. The ælfs barely had time to leave their tents before they were struck, folded and packed out of sight... all except one. I didn't need the soldier to push me towards the cookfire burning beside the last pavillion. I'd hardly realized how hungry I was until I saw the fat (relatively speaking) ælf-cook packing unidentifiable foodstuffs into his saddlebags. It had been two days since my last bowl of Panopticon porridge (which I've somehow begun to miss), but my stomach had been too busy with fear and horse-sickness to feel its emptiness. Two days of running and rib-bruising riding works up a mighty appetite – one which was sorely disappointed. I have no idea how the cook kept any flesh on his bones, if what he served was usual breakfast fare: limp, bland greens gone bad between the garden and the camp, paired with tough, oversalted jerky, somehow gone off as well.

My hands were still tied behind my back; the cook handed

it to my guard, who proceeded to feed me – or rather, force feed me. I sputtered in protest as I took the first bite… but once I got a taste of the foreign stuff, it became necessary. The guard let me wash it down with a swig from his canteen, but that hardly made it better. I didn't think you could foul water, but somehow they'd managed to give it a biting, metal taste. To think I complained of cold sausages in Raligstae. If this ælfen diet continues, I'll look like them in a matter of weeks.

My hunger had only grown when I finished choking the dreck down. I turned expectantly from captor to cook, looking for the rest of the meal. Neither met my gaze; the cook drew his saddlebag shut, while the guard produced another bag from his pocket. I almost got out a groan before it was back over my eyes and tight around my neck.

At least the excuse for a meal was too small to upset my stomach; the ælfs believed in digestion as little as they believed in breakfast. Blind, I was marched away from the cook tent, its guylines popping as the knots were undone. The horses, somehow recovered from yesterday's run, stamped and puffed at the cold clear air. Ælfen voices filled the morn with an almighty clamor. They don't need caffa to stir them to wakefulness like us mortals: they seemed ready to spring in the barest hours of sunrise.

Ropes were tied, and, hanging just as painfully from the back of someone's saddle, we were off with another *fiery-thunder* cry. The ground dipped, then leveled off as we turned to the southeast. The animal reached its terrible pace at the foot of the rise. Once more, it didn't slow all day. I only think it survived because the miles were so mercifully few, though to me every one was like being dangled over the Arch-fires. I thought back (when I was still able) to how excited I'd been to leave Northwall on that cold morning half a month ago. I'd been expecting a pleasant walking trip 'cross country in my naïvety. I tried to picture the white fields of Ælfal passing underfoot; the blind hid the frontier's beauty behind an itchy haze.

The journey felt like it might never end, yet it was over before it began. A few hours into the ride, the soldier ahead of us cried out; something between an ælf-word and a whistle. The soldiers behind matched it, letting it fall in pitch as it went back then rise again as it rolled forward. Somewhere in the dim unseen, a matching call returned from the outer guards: posted 'round the city to ward off intruders. The signal must've kept their bows (or whatever strange weapons they held) from firing on us... though, given my captors' race, I wonder who they could've been mistaken for – there are no divisions amongst the holy people that I know of. They're too fond of themselves for that.

We were near the gate when that call went between the guards and the outriders. Above the chatter of my teeth, I heard the clip of the horses' hooves turn thin as they left the snow behind and flew up a long, narrow ramp of stone reaching down from the city walls. A higher, shriller cry went out; unanswered by the guards, yet hardly needing their reply. A loud, metal creaking rose as the great white gates of Ælfal opened to us. The sight was stolen from me: all I saw was the thin glimmer of midday vanishing as we passed beneath them.

Charging through the main gate, one might think they'd slow at last, for fear of running others down. Either the soldiers cared less for common folk than the Capital's guards, or they put more faith in their ability to get out of the way. If so, that faith was better founded than Kirlinder's: screams rose as we bolted headlong into the heart of the citadel, but I heard no breaking bones or cut-short cries. At first, the city-folk sounded alarmed, crying out involuntarily as they jumped clear. When the danger had passed, I heard them gasp in quiet horror. At first I thought it might be pity at how I was wrapped up like a slaughtered stag. Only later did I realized it was because they were seeing a living, bleeding heresy: a mortal man in the city of ælfkind.

Of course I didn't realize that 'til later: the jolting only grew worse as we galloped over the hard pavement of the road behind the walls. My thoughts had fallen well behind (probably held up at the gate), and took the better part of an hour to return after the rider pulled back on the reins and his mount skidded to a stop on the smooth stone. There must've been guards waiting for us, though how word of my arrival reached them before we did, I know not. I felt their hands tugging at the cables as the rider jumped off the horse's back. This time they managed to get me loose before the animal collapsed in an exhausted heap. I gave little thought to the creature (or anyone besides myself), but thinking back, I don't think I heard its shallow, hurried breath anymore.

Then again, my ears were just as useless as my eyes. Screams, increasing in number or volume or both, rose from every side, and I felt I was spinning: half from the morning's ride, and half from actually being spun 'round. One of the guards grabbed the knot between my wrists, planting his hand on my shoulder and levering me forward. I had no ability to resist, but at least I wasn't being dragged anymore.

There were only a few steps between the horse (or its body) and our destination. The waiting door slid open with a shriek like knife over whetstone, and the sounds of the street vanished completely as it slid shut behind us, clicking as it locked into place. It must be awfully thick – heavy, too. So much for escape.

If the ælfs have a word for *slow*, it's probably a curse. The guard refused to reduce his speed. Feeling the anxious push from my captor, I stepped forward and failed to find the floor. One foot fell below the other, striking the hard stone of a stair

– but it was too late. My head lost balance and the rest of my body followed towards what promised to be a long, steep stairwell. *Well*, I thought (hazy as my mind remained), *it's better than a cell*. I let go, and fell.

Or rather, I would've. I'd forgotten the soldier's grip on my binds, but he hadn't forgotten me. The guard swore (this time in Ælfen) as his boots squeaked, struggling for traction. My weight was greater by far, but my arms stretched back (I heard my shoulder pop) and I stopped falling.

"Be yü more cær-full, mandrake," he hissed, hauling me back onto the landing. It was the first time someone had spoken to me since the Rift. Of course it was an insult.

Tightening his grip on the ropes and my shoulder, the soldier pushed me on down the stairs. I couldn't convince myself to fall again – my instinct for self-preservation had returned by that point. I almost didn't have to: my captor still refused to slow, despite the disaster he'd only just avoided. He had many more important things to do, I'm sure.

I felt a wave of relief as my leading foot met level ground and the stairs became a passageway. I had no time to enjoy it, however: the push became more urgent, until it felt like I was running. The slap of my boots reverberated from the walls as twin points of brilliant ælf-fire poked through the pin-prick holes in my blindfold. They flew past, only to be replaced by others which vanished just as quickly. Wherever the narrow passage led, we were going there in a hurry.

By the time the last two torches disappeared, my scattered mind had pieced enough of itself together to get me into trouble. The echoes of our footsteps grew fainter and wider; we'd entered some kind of antechamber at the end of the hall. There was only one guard (as near as I could tell), and I thought I knew the way out: straight down the corridor and straight up the stairwell (this time with the help of my own eyes), through the door (assuming it would open), and then…

Book II

No idea. My sense of direction had eloped with all my other senses somewhere between the camp and the gates and was deep in lover's oblivion when we entered Ælfal. Even so, I struggled as the hand gripping my shoulder suddenly tightened, turning me towards what I assumed to be the end of the road – for me, at least. Remembering every terrible ælfen torture I'd imagined in the night, I dug my heels into a gap in the stone floor and pushed with all the strength left in my jellied legs. My frustrated escort pushed back. In their long years of service, my work boots have lost most of both heels. They slipped on the smooth edge, and I flew forward. My guard failed to catch me.

Black flashed white. Teeth clicked in my ears. My chin, and then my nose, met the unyielding floor. I don't know if the ælf swore or insulted my clumsiness... my senses, just returned, scattered at the spike of pain. I didn't even manage to cry out; I just grunted like the primitive he thought I was.

My captor pulled me back up to my feet. I planted my heel below myself to help him; I'd learned the painful futility of resistance well enough. He was hardly grateful (though he should've been... I made things go faster, after all). A metal door slid open in front of us, and a few incomprehensible words passed between my captor and whoever was waiting for me. One last shove sent me stumbling forward before I could consider running again. The blindfold had not been removed; the world remained black, and his guiding hands vanished before the door clicked shut behind me.

I dared not breathe. Movement whispered on the air of the unseen room. My ears strained to find its source. A chair scraped back, breaking the unnerving quiet. It sounding like a falcon screaming. I leapt back, nearly falling over myself. Whoever moved it took their seat, paying no mind to my alarm. Wood squeaked. Papers rustled. And rustled. And rustled. They were turning pages – reading something.

Reading?

All my fears of torture and death had not touched upon the idea of being ignored as the cold seeped through my stockings and my interrogator sat engrossed in some book. It went beyond the eccentricities of ælf-kind; it was just rude. For the first time, I was the one waiting on an ælf, and not the other way 'round. At least, I assume he was an ælf – I never saw his face. When he finally spoke (many agonizing minutes later), his voice was somewhat sharper and less accented than the others I'd heard – but almost certainly ælfen. "Have a seat, far-mér."

I blinked beneath the blindfold. Perhaps he hadn't noticed my bonds, or the fact that I had a bag over my head; how he expected me to follow his command was unclear. I managed well enough, though: pushing one toe out towards the sound of his voice and finding no obstacles, I put the other forward more boldly. Shuffling along the chill floor, my shin finally stuck something hard and roughly the height of a chair. Twisting my arms as far to one side as I could, I jostled into the seat. My legs dangled off the side like a youngster's at supper.

The strange reader didn't notice. The text must've been endlessly fascinating. Page-rustling and thin, soft breathing came in a steady rhythm as I sat, waiting. I felt a strange warmth spreading across my face, despite the cold air. The canvas of the bag began clinging to my nose and cheeks. A coppery taste began to form on my lips. Before I could speak up, the chair scratched back on the floor. "Heaven's Dome!" he swore, the curse foreign and alien on his tongue as his steps crossed the room, "Yü're bleeding! What did he… that fül guard do to yü?"

Cloth rustled, then tore. The cords around my neck loosened, and the bag lifted above my mouth before I could drown in my own blood. A scrap of linen (probably a handkerchief) pressed against my gushing nose while another hand wrapped around the nape of my neck to hold it steady. I was suddenly reminded of the father back in Raligstae. The memory wasn't altogether unpleasant; somehow, my days in that forsaken town seemed sunny by comparison.

He stood there a while, his eyes creeping over me: studying me as he'd studied the book. "So," he finally said, "Yü're the far-mér – the gräzí-landér, no?" I nodded gently: there was no point in denying what I'd confessed in the Rift. He kept his grip on my bloodied nose (why he didn't just remove the bag and let me tend my own injuries, I don't know; it's not as though I'd recognize his face). I sensed rather than saw him nod back. "The far-mér," he repeated, "the small-man. The sim-pelle pawn in the míghty's many a'scheme. Is that æll yü'd have us belle-eve?" I nodded again, a bit too enthusiastically. He lost his grip as I went back, and my nose struck his knuckles on the return. My captor quickly got the cloth back over the wound as I yelped with pain. "I believe you," his whispered, accent fainter at that lower register.

He turned, grabbing something off the unseen reading desk. "I've reviewéd yü'r jou'rnæl," he said, voice returning to its old volume: a bit too loud for someone sitting in front of him, but loud enough for any other ears which might be listening in. "It's quite güd, I must say." I beamed; both at his words, and the thought that he'd been so enraptured. "Yü drag on a'pace in many a'place," he added, "but e'en so…"

The book struck the table. I was too busy glowering to jump; he sounded like Obris. "So yü had no príor dealíngs with the prahst a'who tük yü?" he asked in the all-too-familiar tone of questions turned statements. Still, I nodded: if he was playing to some audience, then so would I. "And nün with the church of man, a'síde the usual?" Again, an affirming nod. "And the kíng chose yü only for the way yü trævel-ed home?" Another nod, despite the growing soreness in my neck. "And yü've no notion whah the ah'postetes spare-ed yü?"

I nearly nodded again, before I realized what name he'd used. At first I thought it was some Ælfen curse, but... *Apostates?* That was hardly how I'd describe men following the orders of their king to guide and guard me. But I quickly forgot the slight: the way he phrased his question opened the way for the answer I wanted to give: *Mercy.*

Once more, it was the only solution to the puzzle of my survival... though it came out more like *Mursee* through the handkerchief. I expected some rebuttal, but all I got was a laugh – thankfully not the same cloying cackle of the ælf-captain, but just as irksome.

"Whah say yü so, far-mér? he asked, an odd, mournful depth finding its way into his chuckle, "do yü belle-eve it trü?"

Of course I belle-eve it, I shot back, taking a page from Brook's stratagem and sending the ælf's accent back at him. If he'd read my journal, he knew that Kirlinder hadn't just been my teacher, protector, and friend: he'd given his life for my sake. *Mercy.* Love, even.

There was a long silence. I suspect he was shaking his head. "And yü thínk hís friendship honest" he said. His tongue clicked for shame. "Yü trüly are a fül, grãzí-landér... a pür, mis-a'fortüne'd fül."

Another voice cut the silence from somewhere up above; a woman's voice, so accented I could hardly understand it. "That's ínough, Mage'llùs."

Magellus agreed. He removed the makeshift bandage from my nose as he rose, his footsteps receding towards the door. I felt a warmth running from my nose again, but I ignored it. *That's all?* I asked. After all my imagination had conjured, I was sorely disappointed.

The footsteps stopped. "Of cour-se that's all," he said,

pointing (I assumed) toward the unseen council listening in, "They all knew yü were inn'osent from the start. They simplah didn-ot know if yü were líving." His boots shuffled again. *Was I free to go?* I managed to spit out.

He stopped, then laughed again... more bitter than the last time. "Afraid not," he answered; sharp, simple, and very unælfen. "Yü've seen bah-yond the Ælfal gates – walk-ed ín her halls. Yü cæn ne'er now leave, mortal. 'tis the law, sacr-ed and trü. Faith and græce."

Græce and Faith rose in answer behind me. I barely heard it. I was already standing, ready to give my opinion of his law (hardly *sacr-ed* or *trü*) when the door screached open and my guard rushed in. It didn't matter that I hadn't seen the gates, much less the inside of the city; a pair of far less gentle hands seized my shoulders, and this time, I did struggle. I kicked and pitched and tried to get away. Above the clamor, I could've sworn I heard someone whisper *sorry* from the direction of the door. It was the last kind word I've heard.

Another set of boots came running from the antechamber, another set of grasping hands behind them. Both guards grabbed my arms above the elbows and lifted me off the floor. My legs flailed, useless though it was; I must've looked like the piglet, trying to escape Kirlinder's knife.

I snapped my head side to side as the guards hauled me from the room. The bag, still untied, flew free and sailed a good distance before landing on the stones with a wet slap. Steel doors in a round stone wall, heavily barred and painted with Ælfen characters in alarming red and yellow, met my eyes. I could not read a one, yet the warning was clear. If what waited behind them was anything like Magellus, they were well deserved.

My first glimpse of Ælfal (the first glimpse of any mortal, as far as I know) sapped all my will to run. Perhaps it was the windowless room, reminding me how deep within the city I was. Perhaps it was the apparent strength of the pale stone walls or the dark, iron pillars staining them a dull red with all the years they've held their prisoners fast. Or perhaps it was the holiness of it all; the dungeons were so sacred that I was condemned to die for having the audacity to be dragged into them. If so, then *holiness* looks 'bout the same as everything else... though maybe a bit cleaner than most prisons.

The guards dragged me to the passage at the far end of the antechamber like a child unwilling to be abed. The walls fell in so three could only barely walk abreast, and the ceiling was so low that they could've run their fingers along it. The corridor stretched out before us, an endless line of steel doors in bone-cold stone broken only by rotten-looking metal columns. To my amusement, I saw the numbered rooms had returned in their most fitting form.

We stopped. We turned. We faced a door halfway down the hall. Its number had been scratched on by some ælf too busy and careless for the task. My boots returned to the ground. Keys jangled on a steel hoop large enough to make a crown. One guard turned to me, and the ropes fell away completely. My hands went to my sides, all strength gone. The door clicked, squeaked, *screamed*, and pulled open on a dismal room just wide enough for the steel cot on one wall and the chamber pot sitting opposite.

If there was ever a moment to bolt for the stairs, that was it. But I knew then there was no hope: not for me, not for escape, and certainly not for Alexi, wherever he was. The darkness of the cell swallowed me; I don't remember stepping through the door, or even being pushed. One moment I looked into the blackness, the next I was a part of it. I turned for one last look into the hall, only to see the little square of light was already growing thin.

Before it vanished, one of the soldiers reached behind his back to grab something. A moment later, this little red

Book II

notebook, on whose final page I now write, plopped to the floor at my feet. An ink-pen was tucked between its covers.

I looked up to say thank you. Door 63 slammed shut.

~ælfal's holy writ dictates no mortal (human – dwarfish – outerlier – half-ælf – abomination) may enter the city and live to see the world beyond. execution of this law is open to interpretation~

Book II

VII

<u>Fullborne moon past Autumnal (or near enough) – Day I</u>: My journal was taken with the morn, inspected, and returned. I hate that the ælfs are reading it, but there's little I can do (besides destroying it, but I could never do that). Paced the floor, trying to remember walking the Northroad with Brook. Mostly just tried to stretch my legs.

Not much room on the last page... I'll need Obris' advice more than ever.

Food: little more and a little better than in the camp, pushed through a slot in the door three times today. Considered protest of starvation, but already too hungry. Chimes in the hall – footsteps right after. Must signal guard change. Little to do but pace and write. Sleep: dreamless and sound, even with the stiff cot. Hope tonight will be the same.

<u>Day II</u>: Sleep: same, as was the day. Guard took journal, returned it before breakfast. Paced. Screamed for no particular reason. Guard banged on door. I stopped; chuckled. Might try again later.

<u>Day III</u>: Tried again later. Bad idea: guard took journal as punishment. Stupid. Cruel. Didn't scream again, not even to break the dullness. Sleep: less sound, still dreamless. Woke, breakfasted, and finally got my book back. Won't try that

again. More pacing. Still too hungry to starve myself. *Weak fül*.

Day IV: Lied yesterday. Just got my journal back – someone's read my promise not to scream. Building up a real howler…

Day VI: Can barely read anteyester through the blood. My little rebellion met with force. Beatings only stopped when my interrogator appeared – still didn't see him, blood in my eyes and all. Spent the day and day after without journal. Just restored, praise Fires! Almost out of space. Least I'll have something to read.

Day X: Day ten of Arches-know how many. Thought I'd indulge a little writing. Desperate to hear another voice – even an ælfen one.

Day XII: Began screaming at midday. Didn't mean to: the quiet was too much. Echo of my own voice better than nothing. Guards banged on door, ran in, hit me. Still didn't stop. Finally quit when they dragged me into the hall. Started crying. They dragged me back in and left me – didn't take journal. Hardly stopped crying since.

~he cuts short here. the record of my father's final days in ælfal is divided between the margins of his journal and notes scribbled on the underside of his cot. i was reluctantly given a transcript of that graffiti by the ælfali high council~

Day XIII: Lucky 13! Found out my cot hinges up, and the bottom of it makes for a nice page. I only have so much space, but much, much more than before. Not the only good fortune: someone must've read my notes with a sympathetic eye. An ælf-student came to my cell today, asking about "the heart of man." Told him Brook/Willow's story – hope I didn't scare him off. Wish I knew his name. He brought caffa… think he's my favorite ælf so far.

Day XIV: Didn't scare him off! He brought a friend today: one of his teachers. An ælfen Kirlinder, if you will. Sweet ol' fellow – no rushing around with him. Leaves that to his students, I bet. Asked me to tell the same story. Told it in a flurry, then added the farmer boy's. They both seemed fascinated – childish, even.

Teacher congratulated student: said Magellus had been right. Don't know what *he* has to do with this. Student's name is Alék; writing it down so I remember (it's so close to the prince's I hardly need to).

Food's more palatable, but I'm bonier. Soon enough I'll look like an ælf myself – maybe they'll let me go then.

Day XV: Should've started tale-telling sooner – might be it gets me out. Alék and his teacher brought a bunch of priests (I think: they were all bald as Kirlinder's "apostates") to my cell this morning. Took me to the council. The bag was back, but I was just happy to be out of the cell. People still screamed: guess they haven't told everyone about the human in the cellar.

Sat me down in a real chair. Bag stayed on. They asked me to tell my story, so I told them my own tale along with the others. Thought they'd be bored, but heard a few *ooh-ahhs*. Gräzland life must be as exotic to them as Ælfal is to me. Pushed my luck: claimed I had more stories from the road. Council applauded. Returned to my cell. There was bacon with supper.

Day XX: Felt a bit written-out last week. Sorry. I've a new

105

journal, but not for recording days. No: I finally get to write my book of tales. They set me up in the library (such a place! And the books: endless books I'm actually allowed to read!), and I've been writing like a paper-starved loon. Nearly half-done – trying to come up with a title: *The Serpent Stories* has a nice sound. Found a couple new bits: old legends from up north, maybe even from the Outerlies. So much good stuff! Senaia will always be my first love, but if I never see her again, I may have found my second. Sorry, dear.

Day XXIX: Arches! Blood on the bloody Arches! How could I have been so stupid? The audience, the library, the book of tales… paper baubles! What did I think I was, some guest of honor, some grand visiting tale-teller? And *him*…

How could I not see him from the start, pulling the puppet-strings? Wonder what he was planning to do once my little distraction was finished – maybe that's why he wandered in, to look how close I was to finishing, not realizing I was still…

Well I'll be a cod, that's him at the door.

~my father's hand trails off~

Book II

This book of tales, I dedicate to the prince...

Beneath the Spires of Solace

Book III of The Gräzland Tales

September 2018
grazlandtales.com

Made in the USA
Columbia, SC
15 February 2019